yh

ON THE EDGE OF EVENING

CORNELIUS WEYGANDT

ON THE EDGE
OF EVENING

THE AUTOBIOGRAPHY OF A TEACHER AND

WRITER WHO HOLDS TO THE OLD WAYS

By Cornelius Weygandt

THE NIGHT COMETH, WHEN NO MAN CAN WORK. JOHN 9:4

G. P. PUTNAM'S SONS   NEW YORK

CONTENTS

ILLUSTRATIONS

ACKNOWLEDGMENTS

THE AUTHOR wishes to thank Henry Holt & Company for permission to use some lines from *Collected Poems* by Robert Frost.

He also wishes to thank The Macmillan Company for permission to use one line from "To the Rose upon the Rood of Time" and one line from "Meditation of an Old Fisherman" from Collected Poems by W. B. Yeats; one line from "Deirdre" from *Plays in Prose and Verse* by W. B. Yeats; and one line from "Sonnet" from *Poems* by John Masefield.

MY YEARS IN RETROSPECT

IT MUST be that my writing has revealed what my life has been. It is intimate writing, as the essay has to be, and as the kind of literary criticism I write has been from the time of Sir Philip Sidney to today. It is all autobiographical in one sense, objective though so much of it is. My belief about writing is that one should be so lost in a subject that it possesses him and makes him forget everything but what he is writing about. I have never had much patience with self-expression as an end in writing. What I have written about is this, that, and the other thing that has possessed me since childhood. The chapters of autobiography in *Tuesdays at Ten, The Red Hills, The Wissahickon Hills, A Passing America, The White Hills, The Blue Hills, New Hampshire Neighbors, Philadelphia Folks, The Dutch Country, Down Jersey, November Rowen, The Plenty of Pennsylvania,* and *The Heart of New Hampshire,* and the chapters that record my reading and thinking, *Irish Plays and Playwrights, A Century of the English Novel, The Time of Tennyson,* and *The Times of Yeats,* are not, however, correlated with my daily living in these books. That is what I am trying to do here, to give the background from which the books evolved.

Mine has been a typical American life of a Pennsylvanian who was born in post-Civil War days, who grew up in a United States liberalized by the world culture revealed in the Philadelphia Centennial of 1876, who was of the generation that rediscovered the beauty of colonial America, and who, though delighted with the wonders of the electrical age, refused to accept the dicta of the age that tried to break with everything of the past.

I have been advised to be brutally frank in these pages, to put everything down as if it were a diary of a bygone age. My father kept such a diary, which I think ought to be printed at some future time, for it is a daily record from 1848 until 1907 of a man of affairs in Philadelphia. I was brought up, however, by that same father, to be courteous, to be considerate, to avoid excess of any kind, just as I was brought up by him to be as independent as a man may be, to be no considerer of persons, to be aware of the crowding of constituted authority. The gentleman of the old school, the father, passed on his code to his son. I cannot play the part of a swashbuckler, though I have certain powers that are that fellow's. I have satiric thrust, but I have fought to restrain it in these pages. I can wield a shillelagh, having Irishmen in my ancestry, but I have not here brought it down on the ridge of anyone's skull.

I have here tried to relate as simply and straightforwardly as possible the quiet events of a life busy and fairly fortunate until its last years. I am well aware that the years overcome all of us in the end. I am lucky they have spared me for so long.

ON THE EDGE OF EVENING

CHAPTER 1

SLOW BUT SURE

WHATEVER has come to me in life has come slowly. It has come slowly, but it has come surely. I say this in all humility, and with high pride. I was no precocious child. A parrot-like memory and superb health carried me through school easily. I was ready for college at fifteen. It was not until my third year at Pennsylvania that I woke up to what it was all about. So it continued to be with me. I had two first-page displays on my first day on a newspaper, but I was just coming to a realization of what reporting was when I passed from *The Philadelphia Record* to the *Philadelphia Daily Evening Telegraph* as paste pot and shears and assistant on the telegraph desk. I was slow to break into editorial writing and book reviewing and doing the theaters. I was thirty before it was given to me to write. I had been fluent enough in talk from a child, but that was but gift of the gab. I could write easily enough from my junior year in college, but that was but "slinging English."

In my first year of teaching at Pennsylvania, a pert Quakeress in a shun-the-cross bonnet said to me that she thought "it might be said that my work during the second term was better than my work the first term." Her demeanor and tones made it certain that she did not think it was much better. It was not lack of hard work held me back. It was a slow maturing. Dr. Horace Howard Furness the elder, under whom I sat as a senior at Pennsylvania, told us the last hour before the Christmas vacation in 1890 that this vacation just ahead would be the last real vacation we should ever have. That was a true prophecy, for me, at least. Every vacation I have had since then has been, as he said it would be, either time for recuperation from hard work, or time stolen from recuperation to do work the daily task prevented me from doing.

My job as reporter took away the shyness that had been a handicap to me. The family I was born to and the suburb in which I was born made possible that concern with beasts and birds and all out-of-doors that was my first passion and that remains my last. I write figuratively, of course, when I say I was born in a library. I was lucky to have had a father who bought books and read them and talked of them, and a mother who had been a schoolteacher and who was the daughter of a man of books. The bookcase which Grandfather Thomas inherited from Great-Grandfather Thomas is in the room where I write, with many of Grandfather's books in it and several of Great-Grandfather's.

There was always talk at home of notables who kept their accounts at the Western National Bank, on Chestnut Street above Fourth in Philadelphia, just east of the Old Customs House. Father had begun his life work here as a boy of sixteen, in 1848, and here he was president when his life ended in 1907. Simon Cameron, who had been Secretary of War under Lincoln, was a depositor, and his son Donald, United States Senator from Pennsylvania. Joseph Leidy, the great naturalist; Henry C. Lea, the author of *The History of the Spanish Inquisition;* and Dr. Horace Howard Furness were others of the bank's patrons who dropped in for business and remained for talks with Father. Even as a child I had a dim sense that we were near the heart of things in Philadelphia. That realization grew clearer with the years.

It was early in life I found out that work was the greatest thing in the world. I was brought up to work at my lessons, at the corner of the garden assigned to me, at taking care of my pets, cats and dogs, cottontails and tortoises, frogs and sunfish. I worked hard at reading, too, consuming the whole of Scott in very early years, and hunting up all the beasts and birds, native and foreign, that I read of in the out-of-door books Father bought for me, in the old Chambers encyclopedia that was our stand-by.

Play was much to me, but I was not allowed to run out to play with the boys in the neighborhood until I had my lessons learned for the next day, my sums done, my Latin translated, my history heard by Mother. That habit of preparing for the work of the morrow, drilled into me at ten, remains with me today. I have to study my lessons daily for my college classes.

It was in my first working years, as reader in English in college, and as reporter and editorial writer, that I learned what a blessing work was. It dulled disappointments; it made the interims between one day's grind and that of the next doubly sweet by contrast; it was in itself a satisfaction even when it was not wholly congenial. When it was wholly congenial, when it was something I could do with gusto, work into which I could put all my energy, work in which I could believe, it brought me heartsease and contentment and delight. It has been since those years of my early twenties what I most loved, work, whether of body or of brain.

There is no state of being more wholly happy to me than the rest that follows physical labor. I rejoice in muscles that have been exercised, in the sleepiness that comes when you settle down in your Morris chair after working up stove wood, or after piling wall, or after potato digging, or after mountain climbing. There is no nervous strain in these tasks.

Talking to college classes, when they are two hundred

or more in numbers, is hard physical labor, and trying to one's nerves as well. There is satisfaction in such work if you can do it, if you can interpret your Yeats or your Thoreau, your Barrie or your Hardy, if you can give to the students in your class a sense of values by which they can judge for themselves the poem or essay, the play or novel they are criticizing.

Just how important work is on into old age is proven by the way men, without active interests other than their jobs, dry up and wither away after retirement. He is lucky who, after retirement, has work to turn to that the daily employment has not given him the time to do, who tackles the long desired project he has never before been able to get around to.

It is comforting to find out that work that must be done, although it is not what you would choose to spend your time upon, often turns up material that is valuable to you in your chosen work. In old days when I had to make both ends meet by hack work, that hack work gave me, in instances, material that I needed in writing close to my heart. Working upon biographies for the volume on Pennsylvania in *Universities and Their Sons* gave me knowledge of alumni and teachers without which I should not have understood our heritage of individuality, that Pennsylvania men were never cast in a mold, that Pennsylvania did not take men captive, but set them free.

Writing, like teaching, is hard work in any writing worthy of the name. Writing without writing in it is no writing at all. That last sentence, being translated, means that what is written without the style that is the man himself in it has no claim to a place as art. There should be joy in rewriting. A man should acquire the power to bring back to himself the mood in which he made his first draft. There should be excitement in rewriting as well as drudgery. There should be such possession by the subject he is writing about that his material should dictate what he puts down with his pen. No man is really writing until something within him of which he is no more than half conscious takes charge of him and inspires what he writes. It may be the subconscious self rising to dominance over the conscious self. It is in such experiences as this that a writer can attain to an insight and power of phrase that can give him some little pride in what he writes.

CHAPTER 2

AUNT RACHEL

IT WAS my good fortune to have my mother's elder sister, Aunt Rachel, as my mentor in childhood. Living with us as she did, from the time of my earliest memories, she talked to me of the mill farm in Chester County where her girlhood was spent, and where my mother was born. She talked of the daily life there, the life of a little country center, of store and grist mill and hill farm, of the daily doings of a large family; of the neighbors, from pillars of society to petty thieves; and of all the creatures, domestic and wild, that there were in the narrow valley of mill dam and head and tail races, the valley of Marsh Creek.

My father, a nervous man, wanted quiet in the evening for the writing of his diary and for his reading, and so my sister, five years my senior, and I went up to the second-story back room shortly after supper and spent our evenings with Aunt Rachel. So it was I was brought up in the country tradition and, though I was a suburbanite for most of the year, I yearned for deep country. I was not quite contented until we had a farm in the highlands of New Hampshire.

My father, born in the heart of Philadelphia, moved out the six miles to Germantown in 1869, and commuted daily, by train, to his work in the city. I was born on "the west side," on Walnut Lane, on December 13, 1871, but we moved over to "the east side" on Church Lane when I was one, the death, by an accident, of my elder sister having given that house on Walnut Lane associations hard for my mother to bear. Yet there were pleasant memories, too, with that place, bluebirds having come to the window sill one Valentine's Day, and being always thereafter looked for on February fourteenth.

It was in the Church Lane house that Aunt Rachel talked to me about the trout that lived in the springhouse at Milford Mills and came up between the milk pans set in the cold water there, rolled over, and waited for the scratching on its sides it knew would be forthcoming. It was there I was grounded in the many details of country life that have concerned me all my years; Sheldon pears; Dominique fowls; martin boxes; driving through fords; loading the spring wagon for the thirty-five-mile drive to market in Philadelphia; trips by team to church and county town; arrivals of fugitive slaves from the south and the speeding them on northward; vendues; snowings up in winter; spring floods; husking bees; apple-butter making and the barter at a country store. Aunt Rachel was the dominant influence in my life until I was seven, and a dominant influence for the remaining ten years of her life, until her death, from tuberculosis, in 1888.

I never had enough of Milford Mills in Upper Uwchlan, the two-family stone house, the covered wooden bridge, the weaver's house, and all the other hundred and one wonders of that crossroads home. There were whippoor-wills there, and night hawks that nested on an ash pile, and tomtits, and swallows in the barn, and swallows in the chimneys, and pewees under the springhouse porch, and meadow larks and swamp blackbirds, and golden robins as well as redbreasts. Father, too, was interested in birds. I remember him pointing out to me my first flicker, on the larch tree close by where the hammock was slung. In that hammock I left *Anne of Geierstein*. A shower came up suddenly and the forgotten Scott was a faint pink instead of the deep red it had been. I have the book now.

Mother rather resented my interest in rats and mice and other small deer and my devotion to successive dogs and cats. She held that love of animals precluded love of humans. It was years before I had a satisfying answer. That I found in the famous lines of Coleridge:

> He prayeth best who loveth best
> All things both great and small;
> For the dear God who loveth us,
> He made and loveth all.

The people Aunt Rachel talked about were only less interesting to me in my tender years than the birds and beasts, the trees and flowers. Uncle Pline always came into talk of the Dominiques, and Uncle Jim in to talk of driving the cows in from pasture. I was fascinated by her description of how Uncle Jim would put his bare feet in under the great beasts as they lay on the frost-whitened ground. The old sukies would allow him to warm his toes if he went about tucking them in under them with care and slowly. If he thrust them in suddenly the cows would snort and lunge up and away with them. Both these brothers came into the stories of blacks being smuggled northward in the days before the Civil War.

I write here in no detail of Milford Mills, for I have told its story in *The Blue Hills* (1936), in "The Uwchlan Saga," and elsewhere in one or another of my books. As I grew older, in the days we lived at 124 West Tulpehocken Street, Aunt Rachel took me visiting in her beloved Chester County, to Cousin Sara Vickers Oberholtzer's at Cambria Station, to Aunt Ann Buchanan's at Waynesburgh (Honeybrook), and to Cousin Eliza Hoopes's in West Chester. Country cousins came to visit us from time to time, Cousin Annie Hoopes, Cousin Fannie McCullough, Cousin Sara Oberholtzer, Cousin Isaac Lewis, Cousin John

Phillips all the way from Illinois, Cousin Louella Phillips, from even farther west, the Mormon haven, Salt Lake City. All these, as far as my shyness would allow, I plied with questions, the Chester Countians most diligently. All my life I have been asking questions, one of my friends declaring that I must have had speech prenatally, and have come into the world howling out questions. Always, though, I have been a good listener. Had I not been I should not have half the stuff I have had to write about. Not only half the material of what I write is from other people, but many of the very phrases I use. I have overheard as much as I have experienced.

Aunt Rachel was full of stories about her people, all to their credit. It was certain neighbors on whom fell the weight of her not inconsiderable powers of invective, all expressed in parliamentary terms, but none the less scathing for that. I often drove her and mother down Germantown from Tulpehocken Street when I was twelve say, or thirteen, and as vigorous and bouncing a cub as ever drew breath. I remember well with what indignation one of my big sister's friends in these years remarked that all small boys should be buried from twelve to twenty-one. It was probably a borrowing from some of our humorists, but I have never happened to run across it.

Aunt Rachel, who had tended country store at Milford Mills, was interested in her sister's buying, which she always thought a little extravagant even when tidbits were bought for herself. The Germantown wagon and the old gray mare reminded her of her girlhood's trips round about the hills above Marsh Creek and the Brandywine. Our little jaunts brought back the past to her and stories I would otherwise not have heard of the chicken stealing by members of a hitherto ultrarespectable Quaker family, of the long drives to church at the Manor, of her grandmother's forgetfulness of the Sabbath, and being caught mending socks as folks drove past from Lionville Meeting.

Aunt Rachel had inherited many of her father's books and I spent many happy hours becoming familiar with the eighteenth-century poets, Somerville and Falconer, Young and Cowper, *Ossian* and Burns, Burns, whom my grandfather had every line of by heart, the ungodly along with the godly. There were old letters, too, in a box among Aunt Rachel's treasures. From them I learned, all unwittingly, much that was revelatory of American life, of the ups and downs of fortune, of how many were the troubles from illness and loss of money, how homesick were emigrants to the West for that garden spot of the earth, Chester County.

Aunt Rachel was in appearance and temperament what family tradition knew as "Red Welsh." She had not the reddish hair of Uncle Pline, which in his beard was an intense red. She had, however, his way of blushing, the blood rushing quickly to her face when she was irritated and fairly flooding it when she was deeply hurt or maddened beyond endurance. She was proud in her quiet way, angrily proud often. Though she had been very fond of her mother, on whom most of the family responsibility rested, her husband being a born gadder and unwilling to face realities, Aunt Rachel fairly worshiped the lovable and irresponsible man of wild dreams and schemes of fortune.

Aunt Rachel was slight and bent more than her years warranted, an old woman at fifty. She was black haired, with piercing eyes set too close together. Those eyes were little and black, loving and inquisitive. As I remember her in her last years—she died at sixty-three—there was always the hectic flush of the consumptive on her cheeks. She was the very incarnation of loyalty, choleric, prejudiced, sharp-tongued, and wholly devoted to her sister's children. What most endeared her to me was her endowment with the country heart. Of country things Mother loved only her rose garden, but Aunt Rachel loved all there was on a farm. She was sympathetic to all my collecting of beasts and birds, though her heart went out to the tortoises and screech owls I crowded into quarters too small for their comfort. At her plea I restored tortoises and owls and a wild rabbit to freedom. She could not bear anything caged.

Aunt Rachel was surprisingly candid and outspoken for a countrywoman of the Victorian age. She thought too much pother was made over men. The world would still go on, and what was important in the world's work be done even if nine out of every ten men were done away with. One out of every ten would be enough to perpetuate the race and women be largely relieved of having men under their feet if they had them in the house only one month of the twelve for breeding purposes. Aunt Rachel would have made a very paragon of an Amazon. Men had too easy a time of it and foolish women were largely responsible for their selfishness and self-importance. She was always quoting:

> Man's work is from sun to sun;
> Woman's work is never done.

The amazonian tenets of Aunt Rachel would have been unutterably shocking to my mother, who had the fear in her heart of what the neighbors would say, a fear that never animated either Aunt Rachel or Father, both of them as independent human beings as even the States could produce.

CHAPTER 3

LAURENCE KELLY

THERE was Daniel McCarthy, gardener, off and on, at Church Lane. His job there, however, was only a part-time one, and though I tagged after him, small-boy fashion, I never knew him very well. Laurence Kelly, who, as our man of all work on Tulpehocken Street, became one of the influences of my later boyhood and youth, was the man of all work at our next-door neighbor's on Church Lane. Then he was to me the ogre who drowned all the kittens about the D'Invillier's barn. After he came to us on Tulpehocken Street he became my guide, philosopher, and friend. He had come from the county Wexford in southeastern Ireland in 1849 and gone to work for Reuben Haines over in Cheltenham. Mr. Haines was a proved farmer and nurseryman, who taught Laurence the best methods of the mid-nineteenth century in gardening and general farm work.

I, too, had a natural bent for gardening and for raising chickens, and I often worked with Laurence, impeding his labors no doubt as he wheeled out manure and dug and raked and hoed. I could help now and then when there was lifting beyond the powers of one man. I was a rugged boy, heavily set and with a will to work, and I liked to feel myself useful. Laurence was habitually a grave person but he had his moments of relaxation, in which he was gay enough to turn cartwheels, accompanying his gyrations with songs the words of which I failed to catch in every instance, perhaps fortunately, for there are folk songs in Irish, as in other languages, naked and unashamed. An Irishman of eighty, of whom I hear often, takes his shower each morning with English abandon and to the tune of songs in Irish with Rabelaisian words.

Laurence taught me many rhymes and told me many stories of Dean Swift and his man Jack. It was from him I learned:

> Brian O'Lynn had no trousers to wear;
> He got an old sheepskin for to make him a pair.
> "With the skinny side out and the woolly side in,
> Sure it's pleasant and warrum," said Brian O'Lynn

His favorite, made doubly dear to me because we, too, had an old gray mare was:

> Brian O'Lynn had an old gray mare;
> Her shanks they were long and her sides they were bare.

I had to grow older to understand the full purport of:

> Brian O'Lynn, his wife and wife's mother,
> They all went down to the bridge together;
> The bridge fell out and they fell in;
> "Sure the swimming is good," said Brian O'Lynn.

It was, of course, our robin and not the smaller Old World bird I saw when Laurence reeled off:

> A robin, a bobbin, a big bellied ben, Sir!
> He ate more meat than four score of men, Sir!
> He ate a cow, he ate a calf,
> He ate a butcher and a half.
> He ate a church, he ate its steeple,
> He ate the priest and all its people.

Laurence would, when he felt his oats, chant this as he turned the cartwheels aforesaid across the floor of the shed at the front of the stable. He would say, as he threw himself over onto his hands: "A rob-bin." "A bob-bin" would be ejaculated as he came to his feet again and clacked them on the floor. There would follow "A big bellied ben, Sir!" and he would come to his feet with a clack at the "Sir" that ended the line. There was not room in the shed for him to cartwheel the song through to its end. He had to reverse himself and cartwheel back to where he started to complete the chant.

The colloquies between Swift and his man Jack were many and amusing, but inasmuch as they were in prose most of them are unremembered by me now that over sixty years have passed since their hearing. Laurence "threw his voice," as actors of yesterday could, in all these recitals. You never had any trouble understanding what he said for the enunciation was as clear as the quality and power of his voice. That I have a roar to this day I owe to Laurence and to my first English teacher at Pennsylvania who used to say to us: "Be aware of your diaphragms, young gentlemen! Be aware of your diaphragms!" The forbears of Professor McElroy doubtless came from Ireland, but from "far down" and not "way up" in Wexford. All my life I have had trouble hearing lecturers in large halls, and even, sometimes, in college classrooms. It may be that the years have brought me some impairment of hearing, but the present race of actors are harder for me to understand than the race I met in the 1890's.

For one thing many of them think it is realistic to talk with their backs to the audience and in natural tones. When one stops to think how large a concession to what is impossible any stage show entails, that we must imagine one side of a room, say, has been torn off and we the audience are looking in on the action in the room so mutilated, it is ridiculous to carry realism to the lengths of the cast of, say, *The Moon on the Yellow River*. That play of Dennis Johnstone's was played by a group of well-trained actors, but their efforts failed largely of proper effect because they talked with their backs to the audience.

I am still, at seventy-four, talking at this place and that, and I seldom talk anywhere but someone in the audience adds to a word or two of taffy a most sincere: "And I could hear you." Evidently a great many talkers cannot be heard. A colleague of mine used to tell me he could hear me through three closed doors and two hallways between his room, No. 203 College Hall, University of Pennsylvania, and my room, No. 211.

It was from the lips of Laurence fell the first spoken words that sounded rhythmically on my ears. It was after I was fairly well used to his periods that Father took me to see Booth as Iago and I first heard blank verse read as it should be read. Father and Mother alike were full of quotations from verse, and Father fond of many of the passages of sonorous prose from the King James Bible. I had heard lines of the Psalms and Ecclesiastes and The Song of Solomon that are with me yet when I was a small child in church and Sunday school. Somehow, though, I did not feel then as if those perfect phrases and sentences were a part of daily life. The "beautiful speaking" of Laurence was a part of life. Through much association with him the lilt of the Elizabethan-like English of Ireland grew familiar to my ears.

When I began to be conscious of style as a boy in college, Laurence was still about with rhythmic speech to delight me. We used to sit in the furnace house of the greenhouse on Upsal Street, each on a reversed five-eighths basket, at fall of night, the old man reciting those old rhymes and folk tales I had heard for ten years but never tired of. Sometimes, on mild eves of November, the door would be open, and we could see the long line of blackbirds and the little bunches of robins against the west that paled from wild glitterings of red to a roseate glow. The birds were homing to their roosts at Awbury, back Haines Street in East Germantown. Always Laurence used the same words in telling me of Dean Swift, or whoever was the hero of the tale he told. The tales were word for word as his father, the shannachie in Old World Wexford, had told them. His recital was as letter perfect in the prose as in the verse. He had every story, as every rhyme, by heart. His repertoire of tales reached back beyond the great Dean's time, all the way to those days when the Danes were in Ireland. Laurence held his descent was from the Danes, a term that fused into one the Scandinavian invaders of Ireland and the De Danaans of legendary times.

The little incidents of Old Country life were wonders to me: colleens making necklaces of birds' eggs for themselves; the pegging of mice or shrews into holes bored in apple trees to lift blights from the orchard; the mowing of lawns with a scythe instead of with a lawn mower; the hedging and ditching; the rolling up of sod as if it were carpet; but most of all the storytelling of his father. His father cobbled, and brought business to his cottage by telling stories. How clear the picture Laurence drew is to me after the passage of more than half a century! The thatched and whitewashed cottage with a door in the center and a window on either side of the door. The old man sitting on an upturned turf creel in the doorway, and the group in tail coats and knee breeches gathered about him. As night fell, and the cold mist rolled in from the sea and the bogs, the cobbler retreated into the house, the listeners crowded into the doorway and put turfs under the windows, so that, standing on the turfs, their heads came above the window sills and they could hear the words of the shannachie.

Even to this day Laurence is in my memory whenever

I particularly notice the plants in our closed-in porch. Some of the plants there are the very ones he tended sixty years ago, the night-blooming cactuses for one lot, and others are of the race of plants come down from those he tended, the maidenhair ferns, say, from Japan. I garden just as Mr. Haines taught Laurence to garden. I scribe out a shallow drill for the parsley, fill it in with earth crumbled in my hand from the edges of the drill, drop in the seed, cover it lightly with more crumbled soil, and tamp it down tight with the scribing hoe. That was the way Mr. Haines taught Laurence, and Laurence taught me.

The raking up of leaves and the burning of bonfires always bring him to mind. He used to fill the bottom of all the hotbeds with leaves, covering those he wished to have bottom heat with a thick layer of fresh horse manure, and then covering that again with topsoil, and putting in topsoil alone over the leaves in those he wished to have little heat. The leaves so covered rotted some the first winter and when dug out the next summer were piled under the removed top-soil, where they gradually rotted away entirely and freshened and invigorated that soil so that in two years' time it could again do duty in the beds. Sometimes he would lay down a layer of leaves in the compost heap, then a layer of sod, then a layer of leaves and another layer of soil, and so on to the height of the heap. He trod out the little walks between the seed beds as Mr. Haines had taught him, he put the newly hatched chickens in a sieve with sage in it as Mr. Haines had taught him, he built his shocks of corn against the bent-over stalks of four hills as Mr. Haines had taught him.

In the greenhouse he followed the tutelage of Mr. Black, greenhouse man for Mr. Edgar H. Butler, but he remembered how Mr. Haines had treated star jasmine and

Daphne indica and oleanders, and treated them after the Cheltenham fashion. I used to keep my guinea pigs in a great box in the greenhouse at Tulpehocken Street and therefore had a right of entry there I should not otherwise have had. That used to worry Laurence, who was afraid I would leave the door unlatched some night of zero weather and so kill off his pets. He warred in this greenhouse with the deer mice, that used to eat off his carnation slips just as they would root themselves in the sand of the propagating box. I hated to have them caught and killed, so cute they seemed to me peering at me from behind the flowerpots on the stands, their great ears and eyes and snow-white breasts and bellies bringing a savor of the wild life of our north into that outpost of the tropics.

CHAPTER 4

SCHOOL AND SCHOOLMATES

SCHOOL began for me at four, when I attended the kindergarten of Miss Maria Gay at Germantown Road and Church Lane, or Main Street and Mill Street, if you preferred the latter terms. We walked there most mornings, downhill to the Wingohocking Creek, past the willow-bordered pond on Miss Pugh's place to the right, under the high trestle of the Reading Railroad Bridge, and uphill again past old, old houses, in one of which my better half was born, and on to the old house on Market Square in which the kindergarten was situated.

Those were leisurely days. When you arrived at the foot of the cleated boardwalk to Church Lane Station and the train was pulling in, the conductor would call out reassuringly: "Don't hurry too hard. It's bad for the heart. We'll wait for you." In those days they looked at the season tickets only at the first of the year. After those early days of January the conductor just nodded to those he knew had season tickets. There were no numbers to punch for day on day. The tickets were just cardboards entitling the holder to passage until the next thirty-first of December.

One of our neighbors, a descendant of raiders from the Scottish side of the border, after he had bought tickets year after year for years, conceived a happy idea for the doing away with the necessity for buying them. He shipped a great deal of freight and express matter over the Reading lines and thought he ought to have a pass, at least from Germantown to Philadelphia. So he went to town by horse car for the first week in January, a long and laborious journey, and a cold one despite salt hay knee high on the bottom of the horse car and a coal stove in the corner of the car. He argued, and rightly, that the railroad conductor would not notice his absence that first week. He returned to the trains the second week in January and rode to town, as he used to say, "free, gratis, for nothing" the rest of the year.

He died game. Although he had a business that gave him a comfortable living he would play the stock market. He knew it was a hazardous game. For years he carried a capsule with prussic acid in it. Finally when ruin faced him, he swallowed the capsule, on a day of heavy snow. It was given out he died of heart failure, brought on by the labor of making his way to the train through the blizzard.

We often walked to kindergarten with the children of neighbors, some of whom were Friends. This led to opprobrious rhymes being hurled at us by little muckers, folk verse anent the Quakers that the conventionalities will not allow me to quote. We passed a barber shop just before we reached Main Street, kept by a very black Negro, on whose window some wag had induced the proprietor to have recorded in large letters: PRESTIDIGITATIC HAIR CUTTER AND ECSTATIC SHAVER.

We wove mats of pink and gray paper in the kindergarten, we made log houses of gray clay, we marched to a triangle's dubious music. As I look back on it it amounted to nothing at all, save to take us off our mothers' and nurses' hands for three hours of a morning. Later on in youth, when I knew that the Market Square Presbyterian Church next door but one to the kindergarten had had for its first pastor, when it was a German Reformed church, my great-great-great-great-grandfather, Johannes

Bechtel, the neighborhood took on a greater interest for me than it had ever had before.

It was just across the street from the kindergarten that old Dr. Wister rescued me from a gray woodlouse that was torturing my inner ear. At Tulpehocken Street, playing in the woodpile by the stable, the creature, which I called an armadillo bug, somehow got into my ear. In his struggles to get out he hurt me almost beyond endurance. Taking me by the hand, Mother started out for Dr. James Darrach's. He was not home. Nor was Dr. Downs across Green Street, nor Dr. Dunton at Main and High. On we went down Main Street until we saw Dr. Wister's gig in front of Eberle's. The old physician was gruff but sympathetic. He ordered Eberle to give him some warm sweet oil. It took some time to prepare that and draw it up into a syringe. The warm oil squirted into my ear brought out the woodlouse but failed to kill it. It fell on the floor and began to make off, leaving a trail of oil behind it. The doctor was gouty but doughty. Despite stiff knees he accomplished a hop, skip, and a jump, with a slip on the oil that threatened disaster. His progress enabled him to overtake the insect, and crush it with his foot. That slip on the oil and the prospect of the villain escaping so enraged the old doctor that the air was blue with the brimstone of his oaths. "Pardon me, madam," he said, with a sweeping bow, "for my language, but you will admit, will you not, that that bug was a blank-blank son of a blank." Mother was a most decorous Victorian lady, but I am sure in her heart she agreed with the doctor.

I passed on from kindergarten to dame school, at Mrs. Elizabeth Lane Head's on Green Street below Harvey, four doors from Dr. Darrach's office. There on my first day I met my first opossum, or opossums rather. Lane and Joe Head had captured the mother with six young in the

Waterworks Woods. They had her in a barrel with a covered top in their room on the third floor. I do not know
whether the lady of the house knew of her seven boarders
or not. They were not there long, though, for the mother
escaped presumably by pushing off the cover of her prison
and carrying all her family down the rain-water pipe in
safety to the ground.

In several surreptitious visits to that barrel I never saw
the mother playing with her young. Nor when I caught
one after one, a whole family of half-grown possums at
Upsal Street, and kept them in a box covered with cellar
window wire, did I ever catch them playing with one another. Even to this day I have never seen a possum play.
About the end of the first week of November, 1937, Son
found a possum in the barn when he ran his car in to put
it up for the night. The lights picked up the beast but he
hurried out of the way. Son gathered him in by the tail
and brought him in to the living room, where was Dusty,
the half-grown cat. Put down on the floor the possum scut-
tled around and took refuge in the north corner between
the piano and the wall. Dusty advanced toward him pa-
cifically but cautiously. When he was about to put a paw
out to invite the possum to play, it hissed at the cat
hoarsely, in true possum fashion. Dusty could not take
that, so he hissed back sharply, in true cat fashion. We
should have had a camera handy then, for never again, I
am afraid, shall we see puss and a possum vis-à-vis.

Mrs. Head was a teacher out of a thousand. The school
hours there were a pure joy, as they were, too, after she
moved to East Price Street. She took us to the Waterworks
Woods and to Thomas Woods close by and taught us what
were peninsulas and capes and atolls by allowing us to
make them out of the sand of the bottom of the stream
as we played in it barefoot. She taught us that the lines of

fortune on our hands were there because of the way our hands were folded in embryo. She went as far as the times would allow in following out Froebel's theories of education.

She read us Ruskin, and the old ballads. She had us recite "Tubal Cain was a man of might." I know much of it even today, sixty-odd years after learning it for her. At an even earlier age I had learned "Listen, my children, and you shall hear" by hearing my sister reciting it to mother so she would be perfect at it when she came to recite it for Mrs. Head. She encouraged us to know the flowers and trees, the birds and beasts of the neighborhood. She told us fascinating stories of the Bayou Teche in Louisiana and of places far east in Maine. She had a a way with her with all sorts and conditions of men at all of the ages of man, a way that is given to few humans to possess.

The sense of yesterday there was about the Germantown Academy impressed even the boy of ten I was when I went there in the fall of 1882. In the five years I spent there I met several boys destined to rise to prominence in American life. A classmate of mine, both here and at Pennsylvania, was Jimmy Perry, the Rev. Dr. James DeWolf Perry, who was for several years the presiding bishop of the Episcopal Church in the United States, in short the Episcopal pope. Two classes after us was Thomas Sovereign Gates, who after an apprenticeship in the law office of John G. Johnson went to the Pennsylvania Company as trust officer, to the Philadelphia Trust Company as president, then to Drexel's as a partner, and finally became president of the University of Pennsylvania in 1930. I saw a good deal of Tom along in the early 1900's, a love of out-of-doors shared by us in common taking us together on walks in the Wissahickon Woods, in the Whitemarsh

Valley, and to Valley Forge and the Skippack and Perkiomen. Tall rhododendrons in my heath bed were brought home from Valley Forge, plants two inches high wrapped up in a pocket handkerchief, in 1902 or 1903. Once we saw an eagle flying low past the convent at the foot of Chestnut Hill.

A boy who graduated from the Germantown Academy in 1891 was Mr. Justice Owen J. Roberts, of the Supreme Court of the United States. I knew him not only as a boy in school but in his home, his mother's folk coming from that same Upper Uwchlan in Chester County in which my mother was born. He was a teacher in the Law School at Pennsylvania from 1898 to 1918, and therefore a colleague of mine during much of the time of my teaching in the College of Pennsylvania. His father I knew well. When I met him in his extreme old age at Broad and Chestnut Streets, Josephus told me he had just walked out Chestnut Street from Fourth to Broad Streets, ten city blocks, without meeting anyone he knew until he happened on me. No one has ever brought home to me the loneliness of old age as he did on that occasion, and on my meeting him shortly afterward at the funeral of my uncle Samuel Behm. Josephus was a clubbable man but he could not find the companionship in men of my generation that he had found in those born in the 1830's or '40's.

There is a curious crook of a finger in the Behms. One of the sons of Uncle Sammy had it. One of his great-grandchildren has it. Meeting a man of the name, with whom the family tree gave him no relationship, Will Behm put out his own crooked finger and laid it alongside a finger of the man of like name. Both fingers were crooked alike. There was no longer any doubt of the cousinship.

I have run on one other like coincidence. My own cousin on my mother's side, James Belcomb Thomas of Pittsburgh, is the only one of all of our cousinage with Thomas blood in their veins who has his particular profile. His twin brother and all his first cousins had other physiognomies. We often wondered to whom Beebe harked back. We know the Thomas genealogy back only to an Isaac Thomas who came to Chester County from Wales in the mid-eighteenth century. This Isaac's son Isaac was my great-grandfather and Beebe Thomas' great-grandfather. In the summer of 1937 Isaac Thomas, of the Hill School in Pottstown, Pennsylvania, called on us in our summer home in North Sandwich, New Hampshire. The minute he came up the steps to our piazza I looked at Sara and she at me. This Isaac Thomas had a profile identical with Beebe's. There was no doubt they were cousins.

Another classmate at the Germantown Academy and also at Pennsylvania was Francis Churchill Williams, the author of *J. Devlin Boss* (1901), the best story that has ever been written about politics in Philadelphia. For years on the staffs of *Lippincott's* and of *The Saturday Evening Post*, Churchie retired to a Bucks County farm east of Gardenville, where he rejoiced in a hardy old age devoted to work out-of-doors. Next door to him lived Horace Mather Lippincott, also a Germantown Academy and Pennsylvania graduate, who knows more than anybody else about colonial Pennsylvania and Pennsylvania from colonial times to ours. He speaks of all the notabilities of all our American yesterdays as if he knew them personally, and so he does, for he has read up all there is to read about them and he has visualized them as if they were his familiars. He is the author of many historical books, among them *The Colonial Homes of Philadelphia*, and also of the pageant of *George Fox*. His house, built about 1724, is of the best type of the early Pennsylvania farmhouse, and he has so restored it that it is the very house of its building more than two hundred years ago.

You could not escape the suggestions of colonial America there were about the old school. They were in its architecture and in the detail of workmanship of stonework and woodwork. They were, too, in old collections of this and that. There was a great store of old prints in the museum on the second floor, the room in which, in the fifth form downstairs, we were subjected to old-fashioned drilling by Mrs. Kershaw, the wife of the principal of the school. When she came into the room early in the morning and said: "Good morning, Boys!" we all had to rise as one from the bench and, standing up stiffly, declaim as one: "Good morning, Mrs. Kershaw!" There was a collection of minerals there that was sometimes drawn upon for specimens to illustrate the Friday lectures of Carvill Lewis. Dr. Benjamin Sharp also lectured to us, but in what year I cannot recall.

I got a good deal from the lectures of Dr. Lewis. I had gone on mineralogical expeditions on Saturdays while I was at Mrs. Head's and I made some expeditions with Dr. Lewis or Dr. Angelo Heilprin to the iron mines of the Whitemarsh Valley and to the quarries of green serpentine in Chester County. I began a collection of minerals. I was already collecting birds' eggs, tin tags, and stamps. The collection of birds' eggs was the half of it eaten by a short-legged hound dog called Yaller who visited round from house to house, not often staying longer than a week with anyone. He was the sort of dogs "culled fokes" always had around, very affectionate, very fickle in his affections, an out-and-out vagrant. He was slow, ponderous, and lazy, but he nevertheless accomplished a feat no other dog of

mine or of my acquaintance ever equalled. Rushing off
the end of the porch he propelled himself as hard as he
could go around the corner of the house and caught in
his mouth a sparrow of a group feeding diligently on the
grass there.

My sister and I were generally driven to school in the
mornings, she to Mrs. Head's on Chelten Avenue across
from the Unitarian Church, and I to the Academy at
School House Lane and Greene Street. This was in the
years before, in 1883, the Chestnut Hill branch of the
Pennsylvania Railroad was built. Laurence driving Don,
or Punco, or Nellie in the Germantown wagon, we would
leave Father at Price Street or at Chelten Avenue, and
then be taken on to school. After 1883 Father walked on
clear mornings downhill to Tulpehocken Station, and
Laurence drove Sister and me directly to school most
mornings. There were days, of course, on which we
walked, and we always walked home unless it was very
stormy.

Some of those walks home were under unhappy circumstances. Two boys who lived farther up Germantown used
to bully us smaller fellows unmercifully. One day they
tore a paling off a fence a short distance from school and
made me walk crouchingly under it as they held it between them the most of the way to Tulpehocken Street.
When I would try to straighten up they would give me a
smart rap on the head with the paling. I made snowballs
out of slush and let them freeze for twenty-four hours.
Then one day, when those boys were walking through
Washington Lane back of our place, I let fly from behind
the windbreak back of the hotbeds and caught the one
carrying a gun on the ear. He responded by letting go
with both barrels at the wooden windbreak. Some of the
bird shot might have gone through the interstices between

the boards, but fortunately for me it did not. I ran, of course, as soon as I made the hit, and I was, perhaps, out of range by the time he fired. He was much below me and the shot spattered obliquely against the wall of boards.

It is only proper to record, after the fashion of Sunday-school stories, that neither of these brothers came to a good end. Yet I am under obligations to them both. Under their desire to kill all beasts and birds was a genuine interest in wild ways. It was they whom I saw skin the first beast I saw skinned, an opossum, by the springhead under the hanging wood in what is now the Friends' Home on Washington Lane and Greene Street. It was they who told me the big sparrow I could not place as song sparrow or chipping sparrow was a fox sparrow. It was they who explained to me the mechanism of a box trap. I shall never forget my first rabbit. I set the trap on Washington Lane east of Green Street on a piece of land on which Charles F. Jenkins afterward had a house. Early the next morning, before the milkman or newspaper servers were about, I hurried to it and found the lid down. By the heft of it I knew I had something in the trap. I carried it home, my heart thumping as loudly as was that of poor cottontail within. I lifted the lid after I had him in the playhouse back of the greenhouse at home and he nearly reached the seven-foot-high roof of that room by jumping and scrambling in that corner. I made a hutch for him close by the playhouse but after no success in taming him in a six weeks' trial I followed Aunt Rachel's advice and freed him.

At school the deeply worn step of soapstone at the front door gave me my first realization of the generations of men. The crown of England, shot through with rifle balls, above the school weathervane, seemed the incarnation of the romance of here and yesterday to me, believing, as I

chose to, that those holes were made by the bullets from
the flintlocks of backswoodmen of Revolutionary times.
I liked recess on rainy days, when we were turned into
the attic to play. There were the bell and the rope by
which, on rare occasions, we were allowed to toll it. Ever
since then the picture of it hung there in its high cradle
has risen before me when I have read of great bells pealing. It is its sound I hear when the thought of wild bells
ringing out to the wild sky comes to mind or I hear again
in my ears those lines of Milton that unlocked his poetry
for me of the pealing of a bell over a broad estuary of the
sea:

> Over some wide-watered shore
> Swinging slow with sullen roar.

It must have been when we were in the fifth form that
our room teacher fell ill and we had a substitute for two
or three weeks. He got in wrong with us for not being like
the Jerseyman whose ways we were used to and by telling
us he had never seen the ocean. Little traveled as we were,
we had all been on vacations to Asbury Park or Ocean
Grove, Toms River or Beach Haven, Atlantic City or
Cape May. We did not believe he had never seen the
ocean, even if he did come from the plains of Illinois. He
had us in reading in the room across the hall, the room
to the right of the front door. There he had made me read
Uncle Remus. Now that most delectable of all books of
American folklore had been revealed to me when both my
sister and myself had the measles, or was it the mumps?
I cannot remember which, but I remember we were served
from the china that was used when we were ill. It was a
fragile china with ground bone in it to make it light, and
a red band about the mouths of cups and pitchers and
around the circumference of the plates. Frank Ellis

worked for us then, a Virginia Negro with a rich patois. I mimicked him with some success.

On a less happy day the substitute teacher made me read "Annabel Lee." For weeks after that the salutation of my schoolmates was: "How's Annabel?" While I was reading, a small snake with a yellow band around his neck came out of a hole in the plaster just above the platform from which Teacher was holding forth. I was standing, reading, the rest of the class sitting. As one boy they threw their books at the snake. Teacher thought they were throwing the books at his feet and rushed at the boys, collaring two of them in his rage but not knowing what to do with them when he had them thus collared. We explained there had been a snake on the platform, but, as he could not see it, it having disappeared in the fracas, possibly back into the wall, he did not believe us, though he was discreet enough to let the matter drop.

When we were in fourth form, I think it was, we had James E. Murdoch, the old Shakespearean actor (or was it his brother?) to teach us declamation. We sat in this order: Jimmy Perry at the front of the last row to the left; Johnny Royer back of him; Bucky Vail next; Corney Weygandt next; and Churchie Williams last. The whole class conspired and learned "Horatius at the Bridge." Jimmy recited it first, in his best manner, a manner that foretold the intoning of his future years. He was commended by the theatrical-looking old boy, with long hair, high collar, and loosely tied tie of flowing black. Jimmy was always lucky. When Johnny Royer recited the same verses the old gentleman looked over his classes and observed: "A remarkable coincidence." However, he commended Johnny, too, for his recitation. Teacher looked critically at one boy and at the other, but they both looked so innocent and cherubic that he could not suspect either.

Bucky Vail had an inspiration and pleaded a sore throat prevented him from saying his piece. Poor Corney could have recited "Tubal Cain," but that would have been to go back on our agreement, so he manfully if tremblingly began the same lines Jimmy and Johnny had recited. The old actor fairly screamed at him: "Stop, sir! I smell a rat! I see it in the air," and opened the vials of his wrath on the offender. He stormed out of the room, apprehended Mr. Kershaw in some retreat of his, and dragged him in to discipline us. The poor headmaster, almost speechless with laughter at our conspiracy, could hardly pull himself together for the scolding. After a few ineffectual attempts, seeing we knew how he felt, he wisely said: "I shall send you all home. Report to your parents you were sent home." As it was now past one-fifteen on Friday, when we were apt to be let out at one-thirty instead of the usual one-forty-five, we went on our way rejoicing. All we heard on Monday from him was: "Boys, a joke's a joke, but do not repeat it." How he mollified the mad old thespian we never knew.

It was in the earliest days when I was at the Academy, or was it while I was still at Mrs. Head's school, that Mr. Samuel Wentworth Longfellow, who looked very like his more famous brother, Henry Wadsworth, was minister of the Unitarian Church. He lived on Tulpehocken Street near Main Street. Often in going home to dinner he would join us as the uptown group of us plodded homeward. I can remember nothing of what he said to us but I remember he did all the talking, not embarrassing us with questions, as so often grownups embarrass children. I remember his benign smile. I remember hearing tell of his grave and unanswerable rejoinder to a little girl who demanded that he sometimes walk home with the small girls plodding the same way: "But I never was a little girl!"

Old Walt Whitman used to hobble around to the school when he visited Mr. Francis Howard Williams on Greene Street below Coulter. He never talked to us or read his verse to us. Perhaps he was too far gone with paralysis for that. He sat there, at the headmaster's desk, sometimes with his hat on, Quaker fashion, but generally with it off, both hands on his cane and it beating a soft tattoo on the platform. I was not properly impressed by him, for Father pooh-poohed his work. I began to like parts of his verse when I was a boy in college, finding bird song well described there, wood robin song, and mockingbird song, and the scent of lilacs, and opera singers of old time, Alboni the great contralto, whom Father talked about, for one. Years afterward when I visited the house in Mickle Street, in Camden, and saw the shallow hole worn in the floor alongside of the chair in which he sat, I understood it was that trembling tapping of the cane had made it.

The earliest days at the Academy were difficult for me. There had been a rule of love and no discipline at Mrs. Head's, and the discipline of Mr. Deacon's room at the Academy was hard for me to adjust myself to. I owed it to Mother that I was broken in finally and taught how to work. Finding I did none too well at first with my lessons, she kept me in every afternoon until I had all my homework done, my lessons thoroughly conned for the next day.

CHAPTER 5

FAMILY AND FRIENDS

IT IS the mother's side of the family in American life that is known best to the children of the family. So it was with my sister and me. We saw much more of Mother's sisters and brothers than of Father's folks. Aunt Rachel lived with us. Uncle Pline came to be head of the house when Father and Mother went off to their three weeks' vacation in the fall. Uncle Seal took me off for trips to the Pennsylvania mountains. Of Aunt Rachel's rounds with me of Chester County cousins I have already spoken.

It was from both sides of the family came, though, our heritage of fullness of life, superb vitality, eagerness, curiosity, interest in all sorts and conditions of people, concern with everything under the sun. I can recall no family gatherings at Church Lane. It is from the days of Tulpehocken Street I recall the most of them, Gargantuan repasts at Thanksgiving and Christmas and New Year's Day. Father's family came to our house on Thanksgiving Day, and Mother's family came to our house on New Year's Day. Once in a long while we went to Grandmother Weygandt's or to Uncle Harry Godley's on Thanksgiving, and more often to Uncle Jim's on New Year's Day, but there were only a few breaks in the long line of family gatherings at our house at Thanksgiving and New Year's. There was champagne after dinner on Thanksgiving, but even with it, there were no merrier times there than were without it at the gatherings of Mother's family on New Year's Day. The more volatile spirits born of Welsh and North of Ireland blood in the ancestry of Mother's family were just

33

as efficacious as the champagne acting on the slower tempo of life in the Germanic blood of Father's folks.

It was not often that we saw Father's folks at other times of year. Uncle Jim and his family; Uncle Seal *solus,* his wife left in Lebanon while he gallivanted around the country; Aunt Theora and her children, the twins, Bess and Walter—all on Mother's side—we saw more of. Bess often spent a week with us of summers, and Walter only less often visited us for a day or two. Uncle Jim took me to the twenty-fifth reunion of his Pennsylvania Regiment at Gettysburg. Those days of early July in 1888 were the hottest I ever put in anywhere. The town was crowded, all the hotels full, and we were forced into a private house. It was in a closely crowded street, with no air coming in the windows, and in an atmosphere simply stifling. The man who drove us about the battlefield had been wounded at Gettysburg, in the head, by a piece of shell. Part of his skull had been cut out and a silver plate inserted. This plate, however, had moved, so there was a little space in which only the skin covered the palpitation of his brain. I followed a man plowing in "The Peach Orchard," through which Pickett's men had charged across to the Union lines. I picked up Minié balls, old buckles and pieces of harness, and the like.

One of the incidents of the reunion of Uncle Jim's regiment was a quarrel between a man who had carried back his wounded fellow and that fellow, now a man on a crutch, as to the spot where the crippled man had been wounded. The man on the crutch said he could "locate" the very fence panel alongside of which he had fallen. They would have come to blows about the matter if their comrades had not intervened. The crutch was being flourished in air when its downward course was arrested.

Uncle Jim took me to Anglesea in the days when there

were still wild cattle at Holly Beach, and terns and plover
nesting across Hereford Inlet from the just built hotel at
Anglesea. Uncle Jim went on fishing excursions everywhere. He took his family and Aunt Rachel along on one
trip to Minnesota. He used to send us salmon from the
Restigouche. It was thrilling to me as a child to have the
expressman come in the dark of September evenings with
these ice-packed and dripping boxes of fish from the far
north. Although I did not care for the fish then, my heart
was already homing north, and these trout and salmon
seemed very treasure trove to me from the delectable
lands.

Uncle Jim was a commercial traveler whose route lay
in Ohio and Kentucky and he was always bringing home
food for us to eat and nuts for us to plant from one or the
other state. I have now in my yard, on Wissahickon Avenue, a shellbark tree just come into bearing after forty
years of vicissitudes from the nut. At one of our New Year
banquets at Uncle Jim's, Father was given two guinea hens
from Kentucky to carve. The sharp knife he was provided
with could not cut the flesh from either breast. He could
barely hold a bird by jabbing it hard with the sharp tines
of his fork. There is no meeting of Mother's family today
that some oldster of those of us who were children at that
party but recalls that incident. Never again has so tough
a bird come to the experience of any of us. Nor has any
one of us ever found out how the pair of them could have
acquired the hardness they had.

I remember two trips to Lebanon, to Uncle Seal's, with
Aunt Rachel. I think I could not have been more than ten
at the time of the first trip. Somewhere out from Reading
the train ran by a straw-roofed barn burning. All the cattle
and everything portable had been got out. There were
great piles of straw and other roughage beyond the sparks

from the building in flames, and people in plain clothes sitting about quietly watching the debacle. There was, I suppose, no water available and no use of fussing about what could not be helped. Their quietude and resignation made a deep impression on the child that I was.

I have been always been more afraid of fire, I think, than of anything else, after I outgrew the childish fear of being buried alive. Father, the electrical inventor's son, used to take me up to the cupola of the Italianate house on Tulpehocken Street in thunderstorms. Every once in a while we would see that a barn had been struck by the glow in the western sky, that same sky that was lighted by the glow from the furnace stacks of Conshohocken and Phoenixville. Our house was protected by lightning rods and was never struck, as Brockie's across the way was one Sunday morning as I sat on the front porch and was dazzled by the ball of fire that descended on their kitchen chimney.

Letters from Cousin Oliver James who lived in Rosario, in the Argentine, were events of these early years on Tulpehocken Street. A cousin of my mother's from Reading, he had boarded with the Thomas' in Philadelphia, while he had some sort of job in a printing establishment, a job that gave him a chance to do writing. A rolling stone, he had gone to Brazil before the Civil War, and then on to the Argentine. He wrote long and detailed letters back to his cousins and they were passed around among my mother's brothers and sisters. Sometimes he wrote to one, and sometimes to another, but in the end all the cousinage of his saw all his letters. It may be that in some of them he drew a longbow, for that was the way with him, but he never failed to be interesting. Imagine my joy in coming on a paragraph something like this: "A great flood on the Platte brought a floating island of trees and debris of all sorts to our water front. We went down to see it come to land. As it did we saw a stir in some of its branches and a huge jaguar, a glory of red and gold, with blazing eyes and lashing tail, leaped ashore and made off into the tall grass of the pampas." It was about this time Father gave me Darwin's *Voyage of the Beagle.* This book and Cousin Oliver's letters prepared me for W. H. Hudson, whom I first came upon in a passage from *Idle Days in Patagonia,* quoted in some rhetoric book.

I went twice with Uncle Seal to Juniata County. One year we camped just three or four miles out of Port Royal, and the next year we stayed at the American House in East Waterford. We drove across country from Lebanon this first summer. I had charge of the horse, the currying and watering and feeding of him. I had, too, the job of getting in the outlines we set every night in the Tuscarora. It was a cold and slimy and messy job. We found as many water snakes as eels on the hooks. The snakes generally swallowed hook and bait, and the hooks had to be cut out of them. The eels were slimy and difficult to get off the hooks and into the openwork box of laths in which we kept them. We had them to eat so constantly, meal after meal, that I have eaten no eel since. Father had a pleasant story of coming upon, as a boy, while swimming down Delaware at Red Bank, a corpse floating surrounded by an assembly of nibbling eels. They and catfish, he contended, were nothing but scavengers.

Once in a while we caught a bass or a fallfish on the line and had a respite from the eel and too fresh chicken that were our staples. It was exciting to have along a city detective of Lebanon to do the cooking. A Negro boy, taken along as cook, fell down on the job and it devolved upon the detective. I hope he was better as sleuth than as chef. We got good bread and butter and apple butter at a neighboring farm. There they baked in an out-of-door oven. A sulky girl, redheaded and of a quick temper, made our visits to that farm a mean chore. What was the matter with her, I wonder, and what kept her in her perpetual grouch? What has been her story since then, if she is still in the land of the living? One of our acquaintances here found his way to jail as a horse thief.

There were ballads sung by our host at East Waterford. I was at sixteen, however, more interested in town ball, still played here, in huckleberrying, and in making bird lists than in the ballads, and I missed chances of taking down the local variants of "Barbee Ellen" and "Edward." The doings of one Ferguson who alternated at second base and in the pitcher's box for the Philadelphia National League baseball team dominated the talk in the country store at Waterford. The storekeeper was, as I remember it, a second cousin of the great man, and delighted in leading the conversation around to him.

There were adventures here nearly every day with copperheads, and one man was bitten by a rattlesnake while we were in East Waterford. Only the hemlocks were gone of the first growth of the mountain forests, thrown for their bark for tanning and left to rot, after they had been barked, where they fell. Our native rhododendron, here called deer-tongue laurel, was in its perfection everywhere round about. It had been the undergrowth along the trout streams of the hemlock forests, and the cutting away of the trees above it had given it a chance to develop to a great height. The cucumber trees (*Magnolia acuminata*) had been left. They were straight and very tall. There could have been got out of them sixty-foot pipes for the "cucumber pumps" of the deep wells of southeastern Pennsylvania.

It was here I first met huckleberry picking on a large

The F. Gutekunst Co.   Philadelphia

JACOB WEYGANDT, JR.
1789-1861

Photograph by Reuben Goldberg

WALNUT CABINET WITH OLD CHINA

CLOCK CASE MADE BY CORNELIUS
WEYGANDT, 1713-1799

scale and the bacchanalia that it was turned into by some of the pickers. They camped out on the mountains, where they were visited by the local storekeepers and others who middlemanned their products. They were paid then in that remote town eighteen miles from the railroad only four cents a quart. There was whisky aplenty and most of it of local and unlicensed origin in the camps of the pickers, and high jinks of a mingled religious and amatory nature. Old camp meeting hymns mingled with ungodly versions of old ballads at their orgies. They were accompanied by zither music played on a twenty-stringed instrument that I was not to see again for forty years. Then I secured one from the mountains of York County.

We all still have neighbors, but neighboring is, in cities and suburbs, nearly a thing of the past. There was still a good deal of it in existence when we moved in 1878 from Church Lane to Tulpehocken Street, practically the last street in Germantown to the west of Green Street. Few of the neighbors went to the church we did, the Second Presbyterian Church at Tulpehocken Street and Greene Street. That is the church that Mother and Sister attended. I went only on compulsion and Father only on those rare occasions Mother prevailed on him to go.

They called the church a silk-stocking church rather than the bluestocking church that you would expect a Presbyterian church to be. Sunday school was no more appealing to me than church. It was duller to me because I was pestered with lessons and could not take refuge in reading the Bible. The social side of church meant nothing to me and the feeble attempts at ritual repelled me. I was by instinct a Puritan, perhaps a Puritan by nature, too. All ritual has always been distasteful to me. I was born so ultra-Protestant that I have always preferred meetinghouses without steeples to churches with steeples. I can remember when even most Episcopal houses of worship in the country were steepleless, that at Evansburg in Montgomery County for one; that at St. Mary's in Chester County for a second; and that at Churchtown in Lancaster County for a third. There are even today steepleless Episcopal churches. Passing one time that one just off the junction of the Conestoga Road and the Pottstown–West Chester Road at Ludwig's Corners, my charioteer and colleague, Mr. William John Phillips, said as the plain-looking plastered building hove in sight: "Look at that Mennonite meetinghouse over there!"

I had been here before so I knew it was an Episcopal church. So I said: "That's no Mennonite meetinghouse. That is an Episcopal church."

He would not believe it, so I chased him over to look at the legend board by the front door. He came back shaking his head and nodding it Buddha-wise and said: "Yes, it is, but it must have been built long ago."

I replied: "Yes, it was. It was built when Episcopalians were still Protestants."

He has never quite forgiven me for that, or for my writing myself down as an anti-Episcopalian. The latter appellation I was led to assume years ago, when my boy was a baby. An Episcopal minister in whose parish I lived and who thought it was his duty to visit all folks of whatever faith who lived in that parish was visiting at the house across the way, whose inmates were Episcopalians. He was a strong stayer. They got rid of him by saying: "There is an unbaptized baby across the way. Perhaps you could persuade the Weygandts to have him baptized."

He swallowed the bait and across with him to our house. He stayed on, and on, and on. I heard the dishes rattling as the table was set for dinner, but he still stayed on, urging me to have Son baptized. One of his arguments was:

"Now think how uncomfortable you would be if you had never been baptized. You should do for your child what your parents did for you."

That was not a particularly effective argument with me, for I had never been baptized. I had to be civil to him because he was in my house. It was a bit difficult for me because he was so persistent, and because I knew he had been born a Quaker. I have no quarrel with any religion or with any sect. I have no quarrel with people for not going to church. For myself I go only when I have to preach. I do not like people to change their faiths. If they have to lose their faith, well and good, but to change faiths irks the traditionalist I am. It was seven o'clock before he left. He took out a notebook as he went out of the front door. "I always like to have everyone in my parish listed in accordance with his sect," he said. "How shall I put you down?"

The worm turned at last. "You may put me down as an anti-Episcopalian," I said. "Please be sure you spell it 'anti' and not 'ante.' "

A few days later another neighbor of ours called all agog and told my better half that we were listed on the parish books as "anti-Episcopalians." The priest was game, there is that to be said for him. The story got around and delighted my many Episcopal friends. Jimmy Montgomery, the only Oxford don on the campus at Pennsylvania, asked me how I achieved the phrase. When I told him the would-be baptizer had stayed two hours, Jimmy absolved me, saying with a laugh: "Oh, under those circumstances you are to be forgiven." Old students now Episcopal priests hail me as "anti-Episcopalian," as they greet me on the street, Father Graham, say, or Father McCarvey.

So set am I in my Puritan ways, I was vastly pleased to find not only the Friends' Church in North Sandwich,

New Hampshire, a true meetinghouse, but also the brick church beyond Weed's Mills, then deserted by both Methodists and Congregationalists who in old years worshiped there on alternate Sundays, and also the White Church of the Freewill Baptists near Atwood's Corners. Not one of the three had a steeple.

When the neighbors called on Tulpehocken Street, fruitcake and champagne were often brought out. We held open house when the night-blooming cactus was in full flower. Then we had folks dropping in until after midnight. We had no sleigh but the neighbors who had sleighs would pick me up and haul me to school. Sometimes there were sleighing parties up Wissahickon, or excursions thither on bobsleds. Mr. Van Schaick, who lived next door thought we were being brought up too strictly and carried me off to Buffalo Bill Shows at the Gentlemen's Driving Park across Schuylkill and to Carncross's Minstrels at Eleventh and Girard Street.

On the other side, at Mrs. Taws's, lived Ross Granville Harrison, now the distinguished biologist. This was a place with grotto and fish pond and formal terraces, hemlock-bordered gardens and trellises for grapes, and greenhouses and hothouses of many kinds. There was a cool house of circular construction, for camellias, a warm greenhouse from which we once stole a ripe pineapple, and hothouses where were gardenias and orchids. William Herrisé, the Alsatian gardener who presided over all these extravagances, was choleric and marvelously bearded, a man who seemed to have stepped right out of a German fairy tale. He bred strange breeds of fowls, of French and German origins, sultans and Houdans, golden Hamburgs and silkies.

Ross was a great-nephew of Mrs. Taws, and Lewis Scott, who lived there, too, a grandson. There was a playhouse in the back yard, as there was at H. H. Houston's, who lived on the other side of Van Schaick's just west of us. All these people were what our Victorian day called carriage folks, some of them really well off and all comfortable. I played oftener, though, with the boys round on Walnut Lane, where there was a more or less closely organized gang. Afterward a love of tramping across country and of collecting this and that led me to play a great deal with Dad Darrach, the son of our family physician, Dr. James Darrach, friend of Leidy and teacher to all who would heed of the lore of woods and fields. There was never doctor who brought more cheer to the sickroom than James Darrach. Wherever he was were life and activity and laughter, lessons in botany and ornithology and landscape painting, and stories galore.

Guernsey Moore, another grandson of Mrs. Taws, was often a visitor of Ross Harrison's and Lewis Scott's. There was no sign in him then, at least on the side he turned to the world, that he would become the artist he developed into. In the designing of books, in illustrating and in the costuming for plays and pageants, he was a master, one who was snuffed out before he came to his full stature.

Samuel F. Houston, who lived only two doors west of us on Tulpehocken Street, was nice to me when he was a big boy and I a little one. I remember the gravity of a swapping transaction, when, to make me feel he was not giving me anything, he exchanged an alligator's egg he had got in Florida for a wren's egg I had got out of a shed in his father's cow lot. Until a few years ago that same line of wrens frequented the vicinity of Tulpehocken Station, moving their nesting site from the shed, when it was torn down, to the station itself. There, in the roof overhanging the platform, and within six feet of the passing trains, they reared their young. I often wondered how they escaped the train as they carried spiders to the gaping brood. Then one day I saw one of the parent birds just ahead of the locomotive. It got no hurt, for the current of air driving before the locomotive sliding into the station made a cushion that bounced aside the tiny fluff of feathers.

All down the years since then Sam Houston has been a staunch friend to me. I was glad when his boy come to college that I could bring to his attention authors that were a delight to him. That boy lost his life in the First World War. He had in him that integrity and simplicity and tolerance that made him a loss to the world. Though it breeds businessmen, that stock has blessedly the country heart, a downrightness and love of little things that helps to keep life sweet.

Now, if company turns up unexpectedly just before dinner, and their names have to be put in the pot, we fall back on canned stuff. There was not much of that in the old days and methods of refrigeration less dependable than those of today. We often had to run over to the folks next door for a pound of butter or what not, the borrowing to be returned on the morrow. That sort of neighboring is a thing of the past in the suburban Philadelphia of today. We used to know everyone we met in the stores on Main Street and on the trains to town. Now one is rather surprised when he meets anyone on his station platform to speak to, those few times he goes to town by train rather than by automobile.

CHAPTER 6

FATHER, FATHER'S LIBRARY,
AND COLLEGE

ALL the influences at the Germantown Academy made for one's going to Haverford College. Mr. Kershaw, the old school's principal, was a Princeton man, and Mr. Deacon, the subprincipal, had, as I remember it, been to Swarthmore. For some reason or other, though, the powers that were at the school looked with most favor on the college of the Orthodox Friends. Old David Scull used to come to the school and talk up the merits of Haverford. It was Pennsylvania, however, was chosen for me, largely, I suppose, because I could more easily come home of nights from West Philadelphia than from out "The Main Line." What college did first for me was to send me to parts of Father's library I had not explored before.

I had been an omnivorous reader from the time, at four, I learned to read. Animals, my first love, I followed through the encyclopedias, and through books Father bought for me, like Wood's *Natural History* and Dr. C. C. Abbott's *A Naturalist's Rambles about Home* (1885). Uncle Seal gave me Dr. Warren's *Birds of Pennsylvania* when it came along in 1890, but by that time I was pretty well versed in the ornithology of the neighborhood. Older boys with an interest in birds identified this bird or that for me, Dr. Darrach helped, and I read every book on the subject I could find anywhere. Witmer Stone was four years ahead of me at the Germantown Academy. Two of his aunts, Mrs. Fielding and Miss Stone, were interested in the Ger-

45

mantown Library, a private institution presided over by
that militant lady, Hannah Ann Zell. Witmer's aunts told
Witmer the Weygandt boy was interested in birds and he
got me to join the Delaware Ornithological Club in 1890
or 1891.

That love of birds did much for me in many ways. It
taught me to observe accurately and to keep lists of spring
and fall arrivals, and, most important of all, it opened up
poetry for me. I think it was in sophomore year we met
Professor Felix E. Schelling in the course he created for
American universities, the novel from Fielding to George
Eliot. My instruction in English at Pennsylvania had begun wth Professor McElroy in his rhetoric book, *The
Structure of English Prose*. I well remember the first hour
with him in Room 218, College Hall. After calling the
roll he looked out upon us, stroked from underneath his
square beard, smiled, and said: "Young gentlemen, a bitch
is a bitch and not a lady dog." That was good teaching.
In 1887 we suffered from ultra-Victorianism. Legs, even
horse's legs, were spoken of by overly refined ladies as
"limbs." It was time there was teaching that a spade should
be called a spade.

My waking to poetry came through Wordsworth. I
found in his verses the golden green sunsets against which
I had seen northing blackbirds, and there, too, I found
skylarks and cuckoos, daffodils and the lesser celandine,
that I had read about in Gilbert White's *Natural History
of Selborne*, which had come my way in childhood, I suppose through the agency of Father. What I liked most in
Wordsworth was that he wrote always with his eye on the
object, that he particularized, that he was concrete. I have
had from these early days "that inward eye which is the
bliss of solitude." I can recall much of what has moved
me from years and years ago and have it pass before my

mind's eye. I can see golden Hamburgs on the back lawn
before the hen yards at Church Lane, a tulip poplar tree
on the side lawn full of blossom, Father tying a cat that
stole young chickens to a chair in the cellar preparatory
to shooting it and getting me out of the way lest I be
struck by the bullet glancing. I can remember being
laughed at for declaring I had seen Indians walking down
Church Lane with their wigwams on their backs. I remember, too, laughter at me for calling a kid jumping about
on an ash dump "a blithe and bounding kid."

One reason I so liked to listen to Laurence was his way
with words. Old Maggie at Church Lane had a power over
them, too. She did not like Uncle Pline bringing around
a young cockerel each spring to outcross the hens of our
flock. She loved to bring up young chickens and she could
not bear a young cockerel of her flock being beaten up by
the brown Leghorn, or light Brahma, or dark Brahma, or
silver-spangled Hamburg that he came carrying under
arm, its legs bound by tarred twine. Her oaths, interlarded
with Irish, were beyond my comprehension, but they were
delivered by an oratory that was inimitable, and certain
phrases as close packed with invective as those of Pegeen
Mike in *The Playboy of the Western World*.

Robert Ellis Thompson, with whom we were supposed
to be having a course at Pennsylvania in English history,
had words like the flowing water. There were no picturesquenesses of phrase, though, in this man of Down,
such as you found in the Synge of Mayo or in the Laurence
Kelly of Wexford. Thompson was, however, the greatest
teacher I ever sat under. I went away from his every hour
with a list of books he had made me want to read. These
books I found, fully half he mentioned, in Father's library.
One morning when Dr. Thompson came in he followed
the roll call with: "Which one of yese will tell me what is

a patteran?" He had met gypsies on his way to the station at Jenkintown, somewhere along Church Road, and that had set his mind on Borrow. He talked the whole hour on *Lavengro,* and *The Romany Rye,* and *The Bible in Spain.* I found the first and second at home and was lost in them to the slighting of my regular lessons.

That was the way it was with me all through college; I never caught a condition after admission. I was conditioned in English on admission, on my handwriting, I think it must have been. I have always been good in examinations, getting down in papers more than I knew I knew. I have never been flustered by them. I made more than ninety on that admission paper. My folks thought I was poorly prepared. They got a tutor for me. He was worse than useless. After his tutoring I knew less about parsing than I had before. I, however, printed out the paper in the fall, made seventy on it, and was passed. I have never had much belief in examinations since, though the orals I have given for over forty years are less ineffective than most examinations.

I worked, from freshman to senior, on what interested me, as hard as I could, and for teachers I could get along with. I worked in fully half the courses only hard enough to pass. I enjoyed my courses with Thompson and Fullerton and Schelling, but they were the only three who really interested me. From that day to this I have believed that the lack of vivid life and personality and full possession with their subject in college teachers is the reason so much college work is no more than perfunctory. Seidensticker I got a good deal out of, but that was because I was interested in things Pennsylvania Dutch. There were only six in our class and I could get the old gentleman going on things that interested me. He was too far gone in years and vitality to be anything of a teacher.

I never, by the bye, heard the term Pennsylvania German until I heard it from Seidie. He was one of those responsible for fixing that blighting phrase on our upstate culture. He, as a German, did not know that in English the word Dutch was not restricted to Hollandish things, but was applied to everything Germanic. Only the other day, on the title page of an old herbal, Lyte's of 1578, I came on the word Dutch so widely applied. This book, he avers, was translated out of the Doutche or Almaigne. Fullerton Baird writing to Agassiz to elicit his support to Baird for a job at the Smithsonian, cites his own proficiency in both High and Low Dutch. It is only in the last fifty years that there has been a tendency to restrict "Dutch" to "Hollandish" or "Netherlandish." Pennsylvania German is a term sired by pedantry out of an inferiority complex. My old friend Martin Grove Brumbaugh went around upstate telling folks that if we call ourselves Pennsylvania German everybody will respect us and no longer dismiss us as dumb Dutch. The change of name did not achieve the desired end. My own *Red Hills* (1929) has done far more to do away with the inferiority complex than that misnomer, Pennsylvania German, ever did. Pennsylvania German is a term with no roots in the soil. We call ourselves Pennsylvania Dutch and so our neighbors of other ancestry call us. There are deep roots to Pennsylvania Dutch. They are words of the people, not of the pedants. They are words that conjure up picturesque places and homey ways. They have smack of the soil and tang to them. They do not smell of the lamp as Pennsylvania German does, but of mint-bordered meadow streams, hills of clover, mountains of second growth above white-roaded valleys of limestone.

Seidie began the study of Pennsylvania Dutchland that led to the work of M. D. Learned and Edwin Atlee Barber,

Governor Pennypacker and Governor Brumbaugh, Dr.
B. F. Fackenthal and Henry C. Mercer, John Baer Stoudt
and Herbie Beck, Henry S. Borneman and Colonel Henry
W. Schoemaker. The novelists helped on the cause of things
Pennsylvania Dutch, Mrs. Elsie Singmaster Lewars and
Mrs. Helen R. Martin and John Luther Long. The antique dealers and the magazines concerned with antiques
quickened an interest in our glass and our pottery, our
painted chests and fractur, our quilts and zitters, our old
buildings at Ephrata and Lititz. The Bach Festival at
Bethlehem and the Rose Services at Manheim helped to
spread abroad a more general knowledge of our culture
and of the picturesqueness of our ways. Even Plymouth
Rock New Englanders make pilgrimages to Pennsylvania
nowadays. Our symboled barns and Plain Clothes Folks
in the fields and plowlands and driving their teams on the
roads are talked of from coast to coast. Though you may
meet Amishmen in Indiana and Kansas it is our Pennsylvania sectarians with their proverbial honesty and their
troubles with school bureaucrats that are spoken of and
written of most often.

The Weygandts had had a concern with the higher
artisanry and with the arts from their coming to America
in 1736. Johannes Bechtel, whose daughter, Maria Agneta,
Cornelius Weygandt married in 1739, had settled in Germantown in 1726. Bechtel was a turner and lay preacher
who became the first pastor of what is now the Market
Square Presbyterian Church. It was German Reformed in
its beginnings, and the seat of much controversy involv-
ing Bechtel, largely because he was not a regularly or-
dained clergyman. He was a man of initiative and dream.
He traveled far and wide preaching; in his home the first
meeting looking to the founding of a school in Germantown was held; and he compiled a catechism whose pur-

pose was to find a common denominator of belief that might lead to the union in one church of all the many Protestant sects in German Pennsylvania. That little book was printed by Benjamin Franklin.

My grandfather, Thomas Jefferson Weygandt, had come to Philadelphia from Easton in 1820, a youth of twenty. In Easton he had been a member of a band. I have a book of the music they played, copied out in his clear hand. He had absolute pitch, an ear as certain as a tuning fork. When he finished turning a side flute or flageolet he tuned it by ear and then confirmed that tuning by the tuning fork. His ear never betrayed him. I have that tuning fork and a dozen flutes and flageolets he made. They are to be found here and there throughout southeastern Pennsylvania, the most of them boxwood or lignum vitae, but one of walnut now and then, of ivory rarely, and several specimens, it is fabled, of sterling silver.

In the later years of his life, which ended in 1874, he spent a great deal of time in making what his day called "philosophical apparatus." There were thermopiles and generators of electricity of one fashion and another, advances toward dynamos, attempts at an incandescent light. He never attained to any invention that made him money. We have still certain medals of his from the Franklin Institute. He was a super-mechanic. There used to be about a *Putz*, to be placed under a Christmas tree, of the manger at Bethlehem, that he had made, in accordance with the practice of all Moravians. That has gone the way of most toys, but a set of chessmen he carved out is still extant.

He had brought up his children to a love of music. His values were based on Bach and Beethoven, as you would expect in a Moravian family. My Aunt Sophia Godley had been a church choir singer in her youth, good enough to be first soprano in a choir and to make a good living from

that and similar employment. It was a cross to Father that
neither my sister Sophia nor myself had musical ability.
Sophie was taught piano, lastly by old Zerdihayli, the
friend of Liszt. I was hopeless, although listening to music
has been one of my first pleasures all my life through. I
have all but lost my taste for the theater, but the Friday
concerts of the Philadelphia Orchestra are still the event
of the week to me.

I missed few operas while I was a boy in college, hearing
them from "The Gods" in the Academy of Music. Most
of Father's operas, when he was young, were heard at the
Chestnut Street Opera House. He was present at the first
opera sung in the Academy of Music, Verdi's *Il Trovatore*,
in 1857. I remember Father taking me to my first opera.
It was Beethoven's *Fidelio*. I remember Mother and
Father and Sister coming home in the small hours after
the elder Damrosch's first performances in Philadelphia of
the Wagner tetralogy. Father was never a Wagnerian and
he was loath to accept Brahms as the third of the Great
B's. Bach and Beethoven were his first of composers to his
death in 1907.

A gang of us went to opera in the Academy of Music
during my college years, 1887 to 1891, and during the
early nineties. Those were the days of Nordica and Emma
Eames, the De Reszkes, Plançon, Calvé, Melba, and La-
salle. I had heard in concert the singers of the previous
regime, Adelina Patti and Scalchi, Del Puente, Campa-
nini, and Novara. Father talked of Parepa Rosa and Alboni, Roncone, Mario, and Santley. One of the ties that
bound me to Whitman was his praise of singers familiar
to me from Father's experience. I heard Materna and Max
Alvary and Emil Fischer among the first of the great
Wagnerians, Rosa Sucher, Klafsky, Ternina, Van Rooy,
Kraus, Burgstaller among the later ones. Fine as Flagstad

and Melchior and Schorr are, they are not so fine singers as these forerunners of theirs.

I went less often to the theater than to the opera and to the symphony concerts of Theodore Thomas and of the Boston Symphony. Father, I take it, had had enough of the theater before he had enough of music. So, too, it has been with his son. Father would take the family to revivals of *The Rivals, The School for Scandal,* and *She Stoops to Conquer,* Mrs. Drew's revivals at the Arch Street Theatre, and certain performances of Shakespeare. My intimate acquaintance with the theater did not begin, however, until my newspaper days. With the drama it began at college. Professor Schelling set me to reading widely in the Elizabethan drama. I went home after our first hour in the course and found Lamb's *Specimens* among Father's books. I was greatly taken with Swinburne's declaration that Marlowe and Dekker and Fletcher were "estuaries of the sea which is Shakespeare." I read literally hundreds of Elizabethan plays, taking to heart some of their incidental songs so that I have not forgotten them to this day. I can still recite "Troll the bowl, the jolly nut brown bowl" from Dekker and "Pack, clouds, away, and welcome day" from Heywood.

It was in these years I came on Herrick. Professor Schelling lectured on him and I found the *Hesperides* on the shelves at home in a fat little volume printed by Pickering of London. From that time to this I have had continually an unappeased hunger for Herrick. Lover of the country that I am I was for a while disconcerted by his plaints against his "loathed Devonshire." I came to find, however, that for all his Lamb-like love of the vistas of roof and chimney pots in town and its foregatherings of kindred souls, he liked his Tracy and his hens, his country wassailings and Mayings. Then, too, I was shaken by the candid questioning of Donne, and came to love *The Compleat Angler* of Walton.

Dean Swift I had a particular regard for. Laurence had given me one side of the man. Family tradition another. The Yorkshire Swifts from whom I am sprung had sent one branch of their family to Ireland and Jonathan was of our cousinage. I came to realize his mastery over the stabbing phrase. The story of the blackness that settled down on him in his last years wrung my heart. The picture of life he painted in his satires appalled me. Not until I came to read Ibsen did I find another with such a power to throw the light of a lantern, as Thackeray put it, on the dark parts of man.

It was Thoreau, though, that did most for me, after Wordsworth, in these college years. I do not recall now by what approach I came on him, but I suppose he was quoted in the C. C. Abbott or John Burroughs or Bradford Torrey or Hamilton Gibson I read in book or magazine article. These were days in which the *Atlantic Monthly* was a stand-by in every family of cultivation in America. I found *Walden* at home and the *Week on the Concord and Merrimack Rivers*. I read the life by Sanborn and the selections from the journals as they were published. I liked the tang of the wild in his writing and the accuracy of his description of little bits of nature, like the laying of her eggs by the painted turtle. A white-throated sparrow singing in the night from a tree outside our window at a boardinghouse in East Gloucester made me think that it was this bird and not the veery that was the night warbler he could not identify. The man and his writing are seldom long out of mind with me. It is open country, meadows where cattle graze, and hayfields and cornfields and mountain pastures that are my delectable lands, and not such woods as he most loved. Yet he has had from my first meet-

WITMER STONE

CRESHEIM VALLEY

MAZZARD CHERRY TREES IN BLOOM

ing with his writing a charm for me. His rebellious spirit and aloofness from the herd were in consonance with my own feelings in youth. I wrote the thesis we all had to write in those days for graduation from college on Thoreau. He taught me the romance of out-of-doors.

Robert Ellis Thompson brought Richard Jefferies to my attention. He lent me *Wild Life in a Southern County* and *The Gamekeeper at Home*. One I had, I think the latter, when in the spring of senior year I went down with scarlet fever. I had to buy Dr. Thompson a fresh copy after my recovery. For years I had his copy, but, after the way of books, it is no longer to be found on the shelves of my library. I liked these earlier books of more concrete and objective quality better than the much touted *Story of My Heart*. I have never had any use at all for the "self-expression" or "self-revelation" type of book.

It was in the early 1880's that the old order in America began to be changed by the coming in of southern and eastern Europeans. The only Italian we saw frequently in the first days on Tulpehocken Street was a one-armed vendor of bananas. I never met many until we moved to Upsal Street in 1888. Then they made up about half of the men who worked at the grading of the place. The stone masons were still then native Americans or Germans. The carpenters were Americans, too, and the painters. The only gang wholly foreign was the floor planers. They were Germans, and quickly assimilated into the old stock. The first Slavs we met were in certain of the gangs that worked in the early eighties on the construction of the Chestnut Hill Branch of the Pennsylvania Railroad. We called them all Huns then, and certain of them could speak Hungarian. Old Mr. Zerdahayli used to write letters home for them in his native tongue.

At college most of the boys were of the old stock. We

had no Italians in my class, no Slavs, no Greeks, no Armenians, and but one Russian Jew, Feldman, a man older than most of us and of exceptional ability. We were mostly sons of people in fairly comfortable circumstances. There were a few boys from poor families whose brains had won them scholarships. There was a solidarity of knowledge and of experience and of prejudices such as is far to seek in any American university today. We had nearly all of us been brought up on the King James version of the Bible, Mother Goose, *Pilgrim's Progress, Paradise Lost,* and Shakespeare. We were much easier to teach than the classes of today, classes in which there is no common denominator of culture.

CHAPTER 7

THE WEYGANDTS AND ART

MUSIC was not the only art that interested the Weygandts. There had apparently been an interest in painting in the family from the earliest times. My father's uncle, Charles E. Weygandt, who remained in Easton, when his brother, Thomas Jefferson, my grandfather, came to Philadelphia, was a bit of a dauber. His grandson, John Weygandt, is a painter of parts, and his grand-nephew, Jesse Godley, was a sculptor of more than promise when he died in 1888 of typhoid fever on his twenty-seventh birthday. There are portraits come down in the family. One of these, of my great-great-uncle Jacob, hangs in our dining room on Wissahickon Avenue. My sister has another portrait, of Thomas Makins, a collateral forbear, too, on the maternal side of my father's ancestry. It may be Great-Great-Uncle Jacob is by Great-Uncle Charles. It is in the manner of Willson Peale, though it is unlikely it is by him. Both these portraits are many cuts above those painted by the itinerant "portraitists" who drove about the countryside with a bunch of half-finished paintings in the backs of their buggies and painted in the faces of those who would patronize them.

A bit of still life by Charles E. Weygandt hangs above my desk as I write. It is the often seen twelve-by-nine canvas in the old gold frame of its period. A tray, blue painted, with a yellow rim, rests on a table covered with a tan-colored cloth. In the tray are fruit and flowers little likely to be come on at the one time of year. A large peach is to the fore with two others in the background behind white grapes and purple. To the right of the prominent peach is a blue plum, a Lombard perhaps, and a pink camellia, full petaled and of soft hue. To the left of the peach is a red globe of cherry size but possibly one of our late plums. There are camellias of pink and white and of old rose in full bloom on our enclosed porch now at the time of writing, mid-November, and plenty of grapes still about, and plums, but I have not seen a peach for two weeks. Perhaps in old days they had ways of keeping peaches fresh that we have lost. The camellias certainly are painted from flowers before the artist. It may be, of course, that the fruit is painted only after the memory of this and that item, peach, plum, grapes, and cherry, if cherry it be. From other of his work I should judge he generally painted with his eye on the object. So it would seem when he painted a rooster or the covered wooden bridge from Easton to Phillipsburg, or this or that member of his family. The tray of fruit is legended on its back, "Painted for Emma A. Seip by C. E. Weygandt, Easton, Pa., August 17, 1861."

Perhaps the family business of woodworking gave the Weygandts a feeling for line and color. A snuffbox in mahogany, a sugar bowl in apple wood, and the inlaid walnut case of the grandfather clock by Neisser that I have, show that Cornelius the First was something more than an artisan. The Weygandts back along cared for beautiful things. All the family heirlooms show that. Father had none of the furniture from two hundred years ago. That had been absorbed by the distaff side, as is usual in America. There was a rhinestone set in silver with a cross cut in it that perhaps went back to the pre-Protestant past of the family. It is certainly Old Country work. The Weygandts were Lutherans before they left the Rhine, Osthoven, and Frankfurt, and Lutherans held the cross as symbol more resolutely

than most Protestant sects. I have also a Testament in
French, beautifully bound, with the signature of one
Maret in it, I cannot make out his first name, which would
seem to indicate an ultimately French origin to my Maritz
ancestors from Rhenish Bavaria.

It was while I was in college that a cousin of ours on the
Weygandt side, Ethan Allen Weaver, made himself known
to Father. He was an indefatigable researcher into the past
of the family. A Lafayette man, he was proud that Uncle
Jacob was one of the founders of that college. He dug out
from this place and that many interesting details of the
movements of our forbears from Germantown to South
Bethlehem, from South Bethlehem to Tatamy near Naza-
reth, from Tatamy to Christian Spring, and from Christian
Spring to the graveyard of the Moravian Church at Schoe-
neck. I have been keenly aware of mortality from that day
I stood by the marble gravestone laid flat on the ground in
that cemetery and read there, "Cornelius Weygant, born
1712, died 1793." The stone cutter had left the "d" out of
the name. This Cornelius was a member of the Committee
of Safety in the Revolutionary War and his son Jacob a
captain. I have before me as I write a muster roll of the
Northampton Regiment in which Jacob commanded a
company. It records the strength of the outfit at Billings-
port, New Jersey, November 5, 1777. The funeral sermon
a Moravian dominie preached over Cornelius the First I
have, too. We have not changed much. His characteristics
as set down there are very much as were my father's, and
as are mine. We are hard working, energetic, set in our
ways, as the minister says was Cornelius the First.

Father began buying objects of art from the East at the
Philadelphia Centennial of 1876. All I can remember of
that exposition is being taken there in a boxcar into which
seats had been built, and a fall of water in two great

streams from some gigantic engine in Machinery Hall. Eventually Father had rugs from Persia and Turkistan on the floor, a table of black lacquer with a little chest in gold lacquer on it, carved ivories, a cup of jade, Benares brass, teakwood stands, Japanese prints, Satsuma ware, and other sorts of Chinese and Japanese porcelain and pottery.

Marrying just after the Civil War, Father and Mother had furnished their house in the heavy black walnut furniture approved by that mid-Victorian time. This they kept until their deaths in 1907, but it had been relegated to the spare rooms at the back of the house at 229 West Upsal Street. In the more western room of the two I recovered from an attack of typhoid fever that the doctors thought would kill me. Recognizing Dr. Da Costa one night in my reportorial year, 1892-93, as I was coming home from Wilmington, I introduced myself to him. His first remark to me was "I never knew but one man sicker than you with typhoid fever to recover." The parlor at Tulpehocken Street had been strictly Victorian, chairs and sofas with carved roses on them that would bring high prices today, but that had little value in 1907 when the home was broken up. There was a square piano at the northwest end of the room, the string work on the mantelpiece known, if I recall it rightly, as a macramé, the black lacquer table from the Centennial at the southeast end, and great vases of a brilliant red on teakwood stands along the sides of the room. Bohkara rugs, and what we called Turcomans, were on the floor. Our country cousins and some of our neighbors were amused at the bare floors painted dark brown against which the rugs stood out. The front door that was halved like a barn door to the house on Upsal Street amused them still more. I remember old John Phillips from Illinois remarking: "I suppose you

keep the upper half open to let the air in and the lower
half shut to keep the cattle out."

Father was very much interested in the founding of the
Art Club of Philadelphia and was one of its first vice-presi-
dents. He had begun to buy pictures shortly after the Philadelphia Centennial. Most of them were by Americans
who not only studied abroad but painted foreign subjects.
Our country was slow to believe in "The Higher Provincialism," that doctrine that holds the artist, whether
painter, poet, or musician, should treat home-found material with the art of the center. That is a doctrine I have
been preaching since shortly after I began to teach at Pennsylvania in 1897. It was in the air in my youth, when we
were fighting for the recognition of those foreign artists,
Wagner and Ibsen, who followed it in their creations. Our
painters of the seventies and eighties, however, had, few
of them, discovered there was picturesqueness in the States.
They chose many of them to live abroad. George W.
Maynard, whose picture of an Italian sailor, dated 1878,
was painted in Paris, could have found just as striking a
salt at Provincetown or at Tuckerton, but he did not know
it. Our American gypsies of English stock, Lees and Lovells
and Whites, would have been just as paintable as the old
tinker Burr H. Nicholls found in 1880 at Pont Aven in
Brittany, but he had never come upon them camped by
Spring Mill or Dingman's Ferry. Both of these pictures,
the one by Maynard and the one by Nicholls, Father
bought in our Tulpehocken days. I have pleasure in them
today as I had as a child. I have also Thulstrup's "Dalecar-
lian Peasant Girl," a winter scene from Sweden of bright
color against a background of snow and northern forest.
My sister has a W. L. Picknell with a Breton subject, men
and horses and carts against a bank, entitled "On the Road
to Concarneau." She has also a Charles Linford, of a local

subject, a bit of Wissahickon woodland. Linford lived around on Johnson Street near Main Street when we lived on Upsal Street, and would stop in now and then with a picture he wanted to sell. One of these, I recall, was of a group of poor field birches that had grown up by some chance in a field on Wayne Avenue above Hortter Street. This hillside disappeared in the course of time under an ash dump and is now solidly built up.

It was the desire of the average American who came into moderate prosperity in the 1870's and '80's to build his own house. The men of the next generation were wiser. They moved out into the country and bought old houses and restored them to the lines they had had in the eighteenth-century days of their origin. They availed themselves of what time had done for the old places. With all the old houses in Germantown to serve as models, beautiful houses of mica schist with white painted woodwork both in and out, and green shutters, Father should have built a "colonial" house, but, as I have said, "The Higher Provincialism" was a doctrine not yet taken to heart. He employed George T. Pearson, and built a comfortable house of mica schist but of noncolonial detail that he lived in happily until the day of his death, despite a slowly shrinking income and many harassments in both business and at the Art Club. He had a good deal of pleasure in the foundation of The Site and Relic Society of Germantown, which has grown into The Germantown Historical Society, and in The Science and Art Club of Germantown, of which my wife's uncle, Charles Matlack, had been one of the founders. I remember Martin Grove Brumbaugh talking on Christopher Saur, the Germantown printer, at Upsal Street. It was a triumphant occasion for him. He held his audience in the hollow of his hand, and rejoiced in the long line of carriages in front of the house, the first time in his life he had witnessed such a spectacle assembled by his appeal. That was the night of his recognition as a historian who interpreted Pennsylvania culture to Pennsylvanians.

Sometime in the nineties Major William H. Lambert moved into the neighborhood. He had been in his youth a friend of Mother's family, and he now became a good friend to all of us. A collector of Thackeray manuscripts and of all sorts of Lincolniana, he was always ready to show his treasures to visitors. There was in his library the desk Lincoln had used in his law offices at Springfield and the manuscripts of half a dozen Thackeray novels. After his death these treasures were sold for more than two hundred thousand dollars.

Father was very much interested in the landscape gardening of his place on Upsal Street. It may have been that the nursery from which he bought his trees and bushes turned his attention to Japanese evergreens. There is no doubt he was predisposed in their favor, for everything out of the Far East appealed to him. A Makins ancestor had been a captain of clipper ships sailing out of Philadelphia for China and Japan, and his own grandmother, Captain Makins' daughter, had made the voyage to the Orient with her father on one of these trips. In her old age she was something of a Mrs. Malaprop, speaking of the cat licking her plumage and of the cedars of Zebulun. China was always Chiney to her and Portugal Portingale.

There were many trees and shrubs from the Far East round about Germantown, the purple paulownias, the purple wistarias, and the pink and the red Japanese flowering quinces. There were vases and china dragons, old Nankeen and Canton, in old houses in Germantown, Wyck for one, and Eastern plants in conservatories and greenhouses. My mother was never happy at Christmas unless she had a daphne in bloom then, that daphne that had generally an *"odora"* or an *"indica"* after its name. One reason why the tenets of Japanese interior decoration were so quickly taken to heart in and about Philadelphia after the Centennial was that all the hundred years before 1876 our townsmen had been bringing in objects of art from the Far East.

Old Laurence Kelly was in despair about what he called the wild land at Upsal Street ever being transformed into a good garden, but it was so transformed, and very quickly. We found in the "back lane" a wonderful deposit of manure. Barney Toner had once kept his pigs on a neighboring hillside. The garbage he collected was at certain seasons of the year too plentiful to be consumed by the hogs. He had buried it in a long trench, in which it had rotted away to a fertilizer that brought us wonderful crops for years. I had long a silver spoon that came out of this trench, it having been thrown out of some Germantown kitchen with the "slop." Father had planted out a number of fruit trees, pears chiefly, but some apples and peaches and an apricot that was a glory of soft pink when mid-April rolled around. Mother had a most successful rose garden here, especially of tea roses, and old Laurence did better with the low greenhouse here than with the high one at Tulpehocken Street. There was plenty of manure here for use all over the place from two horses, a cow, forty hens, and the inexhaustible trench.

It was more a country place here than the place on Tulpehocken had been. We had a springhouse, for the thatching of whose roof we had to go far afield to find a man "able for the job." The stream from this was mint bordered and filled with watercress where it broadened into shallows. There were half a dozen great chestnut trees. From the one in the garden I one year garnered a whole bushel of nuts. On that thin soil that had gained for this westward-facing slope the name of "Poverty Hill," mushrooms found what they needed for sustenance. I remember circles of them breaking up through hoarfrost on October mornings. My greatest plunder was twelve quarts of them at one picking. We had mulberries here, too, white mulberries, and mazzard cherries, some of them with fruit almost as large as the bloodhearts and oxhearts from which they were descended, and wild black raspberries and wild blackberries as well as the cultivated red and black fruit in the garden. I have never met celery so good as that Laurence raised. He had the recipe for the concoction of manure that brought it to bleaching crisp and tender, from Mr. Reuben Haines, of Cheltenham.

All winter long we had vegetables from that garden. The celery was covered in under leaves, kept dry by wide boards. Parsnips were allowed to freeze in the ground, but leaves spread over them and held in place by brush prevented them from freezing too deep. Carrots and beets and cabbage were buried in pits in the ground topped off with earth over straw. Lima beans were dried. There were lettuce and cauliflower in the cold frames and hotbeds. Tomatoes were wrapped in tissue paper in which they kept unwrinkled until Christmas. Strings of onions hung in a cool corner of the cellar. Pears were spiced, greengage plums preserved, raspberry jam was made. These sweets were reserved for high days and holidays.

Wild creatures were well established here. Rabbits found plenty of cover in the briar patches behind the garden. Opossums inhabited the great woodpiles back of the stable. I caught seven varieties of mice and shrews and moles in traps Samuel N. Rhoads gave me that his collections might be enlarged. I caught meadow mice and pine mice, white-bellied mice and jumping mice, moles and star-nosed moles and shrew moles. There were red squirrels about and an occasional gray; there were flying squirrels in the red maple by the path to the garden. A muskrat filled up the French drain that took the water from the low ground on Pelham Road, making a little pond for himself to disport in.

The place was a very paradise for birds. There was shelter of all sorts, blackberry patches, a hillside of redtop, spicewood bushes and willows along a stream, a cedarlined old lane, planted beds of Japanese cypresses, high oaks and chestnuts, a cow lot and a vegetable garden. There were screech owls resident here and little sparrow hawks, night herons and night hawks that passed over, woodcock and whippoorwills in the spring holes during migration, visiting crows, flickers and hairy woodpeckers and downies in the decaying chestnut stubs, robins and wood robins and catbirds, brown thrashers and house wrens, wood pewees and scarlet tanagers, song sparrows and field sparrows and chipping sparrows. The yellow-billed cuckoo nested year after year in young sassafrases that were always growing up across from the springhouse. It was while I lived here on Upsal Street from 1889 to 1900 I was most devoted to birds, tramping far and wide and making lists, recording observations of their habits, making attempts to write of them. I read during these years all our American out-of-door essayists, the bird men Wilson and Audubon and Nuttall, and was very regular in my attendance on the meetings of the Delaware Valley Ornithological Club. There were few days from 1889 to 1897 that I did not write down some notes on birds.

After I graduated from Pennsylvania in 1891 I went back to college for a year of graduate work. This gave me some mornings at home, though the teaching of composition and the writing of seminary papers forced themselves on me as first interests. It was in this year that I got to know well Joseph Head, whom I had known from boyhood, and Dallett Fuguet, whom I had known only slightly during the two years we were fellow undergraduates at Pennsylvania. They were fellow students in graduate courses.

There was good furniture come down to us through my mother's family. The Empire desk in which Grandfather Morgan Jones Thomas kept his books, as his father, Isaac, had before him, is one such piece. From my point of view Empire pieces cannot compare to Hepplewhite or Chippendale, or even to Sheraton, but it can be said for this secretary desk that it is good of its kind. In my childhood it stood in the second-story back room on Tulpehocken Street with more of Grandfather's books in it than it has now. Aunt Rachel distributed these books among her nieces and nephews, giving me, as a bookish boy, first choice for my share. I took the poetry, the little two-volume Burns, the *Ossian,* the Thomson's *Seasons,* the Somerville and Shenstone and Gray, the Blair and Young and Cowper.

Grandfather Thomas was devoted to Burns. Album verses of his in the Scots of Robbie survive. The old gentleman had a gift for pleasantly familiar rhymes and a flowing style of an Old World sort in prose. He had a good deal of courtliness in him, always going for his daughters to bring them home from whatever functions they were attending. He was to the crowd a clerical-looking person, being once refused admission to Girard College on the grounds that he must be a minister. Why a military-looking cloak he affected should have been taken as the badge of the cleric I do not know. After he had allowed the milling business at Milford Mills to slip through his hands he taught school at the house to which he removed from the

corners, the house to the left about half a mile from Milford on the road to The Eagle. After removing, in 1847, to
Philadelphia, he had a job teaching at The Falls of Schuylkill, walking out from the city and back each day.

The ball-and-claw drop-leaf table in mahogany that had
come to the Reeds, my mother's mother's people, from
Uncle Israel Davis of Chester Valley, is the best heirloom
I have from the Thomas-Reed side. Uncle Israel's silver
was divided half and half to his and his wife's people.
Mother borrowed that which went to the Harris' from
their descendants the McElduffs and had the service com-
pleted by reproductions. My sister has that silver now, two
old pieces and two new. Aunt Ann Buchanan, my grandmother Thomas' sister, who still kept alive the feud that
division of the Davis spoil had engendered, did not like
Mother's "knuckling under" to the McElduffs by getting
the loan of those pieces. Like Aunt Rachel, Great-Aunt
Ann believed stoutly in family feuds.

It may be that the urge to write that developed in me
during these years at Upsal Street, 1889-1900, came from
Grandfather Thomas, or from Jacob Weygandt and Cornelius Nowlane Weygandt, my great-great-grandfather and
great-grandfather, newspapermen of Easton, or it may have
been more immediate. Father kept a diary from the time
he was a boy of sixteen, in 1848, to his death in February
of 1907. There is no attempt at "writing" in it. It is a detailed and restrained and unadorned record of the day's
doings. There are reflections in it, but not many of them.
Its greatest value lies in its candid statement of a typically
American life of its time, 1848-1907, of what passed before
the eyes of a boy who entered a bank as little more than an
office boy and rose to be president. He always set great
store on literature; he had a library of some three thousand volumes; he was delighted when his son got articles

into the *Atlantic, Lippincott's,* and other magazines. This was after my trip to the British Isles in 1902. He was proud to have W. B. Yeats in his house in 1903, and to have him lecture there to The Science and Art Club of Germantown. This was on December fifteenth, as an engraved invitation filled in in my mother's delicate and up and down and most legible handwriting informs me as it lies on the desk before me.

When I gave a copy of my first book, *Irish Plays and Playwrights* (1913), to Mrs. John McIlhenny, our neighbor across the way on Upsal Street, there were tears in her eyes as she said: "Would that not have been a pleasure to your mother and father?" It was but another illustration of my slowness in coming to this and that. I was thirty before there was "writing" in my writing. I was forty when in 1912 I finished that first book. I was forty-one when it was published. It may be that it was the weight of work on me as a teacher, the necessity of doing hack work to make both ends meet, and that I had to wait until the times gave me a public for the kind of thing I wanted to write that held up my progress. The essay, though, has nearly always come out of the accumulated experience that is rarely possible before middle age. I am an essayist, even my literary criticism has the personal touch. There is a familiar quality to my writing about out-of-doors and antiques and objects of folk culture, fox horns say, or illuminated lettering, or the rose as a motive in the household art of the Pennsylvania Dutch.

My colleague, W. E. Lingelbach, always insists that my treatment of what is passing from our civilization is history. That may be so. I am always concrete, all my writing is with my eye on the object, I labor painfully to "get things right," but the object is never only to record what I have found. I always strive to bring it instantly before the reader by visualizing it for him. There is a rhythm comes into my writing at its best. I always strive to find what is beautiful in what I describe. To me literature is the art of making something beautiful in words out of one's experience or dream of life. When I am told I have helped in *The Red Hills* to lift an inferiority complex from those of the Pennsylvania Dutch under its blight, or that *The Red Hills* has brought back the symbols to the barns of Pennsylvania Dutchland, I always of necessity say: "Thank you!" I am glad if I have, but I am gladder of reviews that find beauty in my description of a barn full of beasts on a winter night, and in my description of the ice storm in *The Wissahickon Hills*. Better still, I like them to quote sentences from my writing such as: "Man has no shadow in the dawn" and "The short morrow may be as sweet as the long yesterday."

CHAPTER 8

MY DEBT TO WORDSWORTH

IT WAS Wordsworth, as I have said, led me to a love of poetry. I read him first in the little book of cullings from the great mass of his writings, in the *Poems of Wordsworth* "chosen and edited by Matthew Arnold." I often turn today to that volume in the Golden Treasury Series, a volume you can slip in your pocket. It was bought by my father, who in his careful way wrote in it on the day of purchase, "C. N. Weygandt Oct. 10, 1879." It came to me after my father's death in 1907 and it has often gone afield with me, in my pocket, as many lines from it for all the years since I was a boy in college have gone with me in my memory. It opens to page 131 to "Expostulation and Reply." On the next page, page 132, you find "The Tables Turned: An Evening Scene on the Same Subject."

The Wordsworth anthology opens to these verses because it was these verses I devoured as a boy. From them I discovered that poetry was concerned with what concerned me, with the out-of-doors that was nearly all to me in boyhood, and that has been one of the seven dominant interests of my life. There was in childhood besides this out-of-doors, pets and horses and other livestock, and that love of people and books that developed into my life work. Now, of course, my family is my first interest; my daily work here at Pennsylvania, interpreting literature and trying to write, my second interest; meeting people, "the proper study of mankind is man," my third dominant interest; out-of-doors a fourth dominant interest. Music much concerns me, and is, perhaps, my fifth interest. I have not missed many concerts of the Philadelphia Orchestra for over thirty years. The cultures of all the seven peoples that blended in old times to make our state what it is are deeply interesting to me. I have traveled all over the state visiting places and collecting information and articles that explain these cultures, Hollandish, Swedish, British Quaker, Pennsylvania Dutch, Scotch-Irish, New Englandish along our northern border, and Virginian in the southwestern corner of the state. Antiquing is the seventh interest.

Getting back now from that tangent, to the verses of Wordsworth. "Expostulation and Reply" revealed to me what joys there were in the commonest things:

> The eye—it cannot choose but see;
> We cannot bid the ear be still;
> Our bodies feel, where'er they be,
> Against, or with our will.

"The Tables Turned" lighted up all the world for me with its pronouncement:

> Come forth into the light of things
> Let Nature be your teacher
>
> .   .   .
>
> One impulse from a vernal wood
> May teach you more of man,
> Of moral evil and of good
> Than all the sages can.

Other moments of vision came to me from "To the Rose Upon the Rood of Time" of Yeats, and from the seventy-third sonnet of Shakespeare. From the former I came to find:

> In all poor foolish things that live a day
> Eternal beauty wandering on her way;

and in the latter I learned to have joy in inevitability of

phrase, in lordship of language, in aching realization of
beauty, and in profound truth as to the realities of things:

> That time of year thou mayst in me behold,
> When yellow leaves, or none or few, do hang
> Upon those boughs which shake against the cold,
> Bare ruined choirs, where late the sweet birds sang.

Moments of vision came to me, too, from the prose of
Ecclesiastes and Emerson's essays; the august periods of
Hardy's *Return of the Native;* and in the famous twenty-
fifth chapter of George Borrow's *Lavengro.* Do you all
know that heartening paean? Jasper Petulengro is speaking:

> There's night and day, brother, both sweet things;
> sun, moon and stars, brother, all sweet things: there's
> likewise a wind on the heath. Life is very sweet,
> brother; who would wish to die.

My Moravian ancestry made it inevitable that Johann
Sebastian Bach was a household god. It was inevitable, too,
that there was much talk of Beethoven and playing of Beethoven in as musical a family as was my father's. My father
was slow to welcome Wagner but his son fell captive to
each succeeding opera, as he had a chance to hear it. *Tann-
häuser* rapt me clean out of myself when I was a boy in
college, and those trombone calls of "The Pilgrim Chorus"
still seem to me to be the very quintessence of romance.
Wartburg and the Thüringer Wald call me as surely as
Alps and Pyrenees and Apennines. It must be that Saxon
ancestors of mine lived in the shadow of the castle of Wartburg's walls, so wholly does the music possess and enthrall
me. *Tristan und Isolde* I have heard sung ten times, and
the *Vorspiel* and *Liebestod* again and again in presenta-
tion by orchestra alone. There is no music stirs me more
profoundly. It throbs with the eternal restlessness of life,

it is burdened with love and with sorrow, it is quick at the end with a brave and quiet resignation to fate.

There is beauty so poignant there is sufficiency in it. The beauty of the *Liebestod* is such a beauty. There is sadness, too, in the larghetto of Beethoven's Concerto in D major for Violin and Orchestra, but it is a healing and a reconciling sadness. Boy though he was, Yehudi Menuhin had a knowledge of the tears of things. Bach's "Sweet Death" voices a grave triumph over the ancient enemy. The calls on the French horns in the last movement of Brahms' C Minor Symphony lift my heart, though, more than any other music I know. There is full acceptance of the human lot, of all its baffling disappointments and ironies and defeats, but those horn calls toward the close cry defiance to all powers of darkness and are in themselves so beautiful, so brimful of the joy of height and rare air and alpine radiance that they fill you listening with gladness and delight.

There is great happiness in companionship and talk, in meeting people. It has been my fortune to meet some distinguished people, particularly artists who have made things beautiful in words. I might tell you of talk with the Irish poet Yeats as we walked on an afternoon of eerie light by the waters of Coole, and saw the great white birds he has sung so nobly in "The Wild Swans at Coole." I might talk to you of spirited talk with John Masefield, and of discussion into the small hours with Robert Frost, but it is of companionship and talk with people who are just folks I wish to speak. Most of us stick too closely to our own circle or group or set to get to know much of simple folk. My researches into the Pennsylvania countryside, my attendance at hundreds of auctions, the way I have of falling into conversation with every Tom, Dick, and Harry I meet that was taught me by my newspaper years, have

brought me contacts with every sort and condition of mankind in the country between the Appalachians and the sea.
It is from people who do not feel that good form compels
them to keep defenses up against all mankind except their
own folks that you learn of life. A large share of the happiness of life lies in chance acquaintanceships.

You never know when what is strange, wonderful, new,
and interesting will come your way. In childhood you go
for a walk with your great-aunt's son through quiet countryside. You meet a benevolent-looking patriarch on a
sunken road in the Welsh mountains. He discourses learn-
edly of rabbit hunting and sends you on your way with a
blessing. As soon as he is out of hearing your cousin turns
to you and says: "Do you know who that was?"

You answer that you do not.

"That," he says, impressively, "was Abe Buzzard!"

You are completely upset to find out that this modern
representative of Robin Hood and Dick Turpin and the
Robber Doanes should be so kindly and benevolent a man.
He looked the evangelist that he was to be rather than the
outlaw that he had been for years.

You are moving a yucca from a bed by your front door
to a border farther away from the house. You inadvertently cut through its tap root at a point more than two feet
underground. The old man who is helping you, whom you
have known for years as an ex-weaver of Frankford, asks
you can he have the rest of the root, what remains in the
ground. You say yes, of course, but you are curious to
know why he wants it. He tells you that when he was in
the West they used it for soap. You have never known he
was in the West. He tells you the story. He was in the
Northern Army in the Civil War, and after the guerrilla
skirmishes he had taken part in as a driver in a wagon
train, he wandered off to Kansas and Colorado. You listen

open-mouthed as he spins yarns of gunfire and rattlesnakes, buffaloes and antelopes, Indians and cowboys. Ten years of the companionship there is between the man who does chores for you and yourself had failed to reveal this so interesting chapter in life.

The man driving you in the Poconos falls to talking to you of a snowfall so great the bears had to burrow under it as if they were moles in the loose earth of a shallowly dug garden patch.

You are walking up Germantown Road about half past three on a spring morning. You have been "on late" as a newspaper reporter. You have come out from Ninth and Green Streets to Wayne Junction on a locomotive whose function it is to take the Philadelphia sleeper from the New York–Washington train. You have to walk the rest of the way home to upper Germantown. You smell bread baking in a bakery below Rittenhouse Street. Your hunger gets the better of you. You scout down an inclined way to the back of the bakery. Two men are carrying loaves to racks on the side of the room. You inquire timidly can you buy a loaf.

One of the men yells, "No, you cannot!" and throws a loaf at you so violently that you can hardly catch it as it comes hurtling at your head. You take the gift the gods have sent and find, when you break the loaf, to eat it, that it is Dutch bread warm from the oven.

You are waiting for Dr. Phillips to haul you home by his car from the dentist's office at Fifteenth and Locust Streets. You have lost five teeth. An old man comes up to beg of you. He sees your despoiled gums. The hand that pockets your nickel withdraws from the pocket's depths a handful of teeth. "These are mine a dentist took out," he says, "at a dollar apiece. See how sound they all are. I wonder will I ever be able to sell them again for what they cost me to have them pulled?"

You have always coveted a tiger skin. A man comes into your office in College Hall with a great bag in his hands. He loosens a cord, and dumps out the richest hued tiger skin you ever saw. It is red, orange, and black, a Kamchat-kan tiger, he tells you. He says he is a sailor off a ship just in from Vladivostok, and that he brought back with him this skin and that of a Siberian bear, which he has already sold. He asks you forty-five dollars for it. You happen to have just that amount in your pocket. You ordinarily carry only fifteen dollars with you. You have been told the gun-men will shoot you up if they hold you up and find less than fifteen dollars on you. This day, however, you had a cash payment of thirty dollars to make. You are sorely tempted. You wonder was the skin stolen. You have the caution not to buy the tiger skin. A week or so later you read of So-and-So's butler who has been arrested for sell-ing a tiger skin from his employer's house.

CHAPTER 9

THE FIVE NEWSPAPER YEARS

WHEN I went to work for the *Philadelphia Record* in 1892 as a reporter I did not know that my great-grandfather, Cornelius N. Weygandt, and his father, Jacob, had run a newspaper in Easton. I wanted to write, to learn to write. There were writers of the hour, Kipling and Richard Harding Davis, who had learned their craft on newspapers. Why not I? Mr. Van Schaick, next door, a man "keen on horses," was a friend of W. S. Singerley, the proprietor of the *Record*. Father had been at the Central High School while Mr. Singerley had been there. Mr. Van Schaick said a word for me. Father, much against his will, took me in to the trust company of which Mr. Singerley was president and introduced me to him. Father wanted me to go into the Western National Bank with him, but he had never done anything to interest me in the business. I had had thoughts of landscape engineering but the love of writing had edged out the thoughts of laying out places.

Mr. Singerley told me to come in to the *Record* to see him a day or two later. I went in early in the morning, but "the Boss" was there, high hat on his head and smoking a large cigar. In those days there were no divinities to hedge a king, no secretaries, no doorman, no first walking gentleman. The office door was open. I stuck my head around the jamb of the door, intending to say: "This is Weygandt's boy!" The warmhearted old codger saw me first and fairly yelled at me: "Get the hell upstairs!" I "got."

Early as it was, Ed Miller, of Pennsylvania's most famous

class of '87 College, was at his desk, the city editor's desk. I approached him. "My name is Weygandt," I said, "and I was to see Mr. Singerley this morning about a reporter's job here. He wouldn't let me into his office but drove me away from the door crying: 'Get the hell upstairs!' "

The city editor smiled and said: "There's no doubt about that. You have the job!" He gave me two assignments, one about a threatened coal shortage, by strike, if I remember properly, and one on "The Peary Story." He questioned me as to my knowledge of people at the Academy of Natural Sciences. I had known Angelo Heilprin from boyhood and Sam Rhoads and Witmer Stone and a dozen others who foregathered there. The next morning I had two displays, though the openings of the stories were so rewritten I should not have recognized either as my own work.

In about six weeks I had "the hang of things." There were about thirty on the local staff then. W. B. Trites has written up the office in *John Cave*. There were a group of young men in that office that made life interesting for all who were in it. Tom Daly was the life of the place. It is always a cheerful occasion when he is about. I meet him now and then in the train shed of the Reading Terminal and talk over old times. He and Sam Stinson were the "Nine Mile Bard," a column of verse and airy nothings that vied with the "Silly Billy," the joke column. Mort McMichael was ostensibly the provider of the jokes, but there would be times when he would be off on expeditions with Steve Brody, the man who attained celebrity by jumping from the Brooklyn Bridge and living to tell the tale. There would come to the office this telegram: "Silly Billy on the office." One wonders what the telegraphers could make of that. Then Tom would be in his element, working off on the patrons all the high spirits that he had tried out on us of the office earlier.

There were interesting men in the office, Old Pierce, the West Chester Quaker who "did" ships, and lived in an old boardinghouse on lower Arch Street, a boardinghouse that still retained its Friendly characteristics. Ned Miller was the city editor, as I have said. After he left the *Record* he started a little magazine. In that Bill Trites printed a story of a man who shot himself. It wasn't long before Ned Miller took the way out of the hero of Trites' story.

I remember a famous walk that four of us had, Ned Miller, Felix E. Schelling, Morton W. Easton, and myself. Dr. Easton was the pilot and down Crum Creek was the neighborhood. I remember we came on arbutus, that Dr. Easton stuffed his trousers into his boots and found some rare swamp plant by tramping into the April marshes. I remember we were all wet and happy when we got home.

That office taught me a good deal through the men in the office and of course more through the assignments I had to fill. It was my fortune to do the first appearance of Nikola Tesla at the Franklin Institute. I suppose his stunts with tubes filled with various kinds of chemicals and illumined by an electric current had about them a certain amount of showmanship, but I was profoundly moved by his performance. My grandfather, Thomas Jefferson Weygandt, had been among the first experimenters in what eventually resulted in the incandescent lamp. Grandfather had got as far as two platinum points between which a spark jumped, but of course he never got to the steady glow of the Edison lamp. Round about in the attic in my childhood were various thermopiles and dynamo-like apparatus. Some of those are about even now and I have certain of the medals that he received from the Franklin Institute. Imagine my chagrin when Charlie Bacon headed

my article on Tesla, IN A HALO OF BLUE BLAZES. I could
have had his life for that. I met him down at Atlantic City
in the winter of 1936-37 at a librarians' meeting. He was
then librarian in New Jersey with headquarters at Trenton. I told him how narrow an escape he had had back in
the winter of '92-'93.

Old Nate Derr from Skippackville was in the office, the
Dutchest Dutchman I ever met and one who "hoped to
God I shall never see Skippackville again. Every house in
Skippackville has a crab cactus started from a pot hanging
in the back shed. Damn those cactuses to hell."

Trites lived abroad for years and wrote a good many
stories in the manner of George Moore, *The Gypsy* perhaps most distinguished among them.

Antisdell was one of the brightest men in the office.
When Walt Whitman died he wrote the local article. It
seemed so good to the night desk that it was recommended
to old Bailey for the editorial page and printed as an editorial. Antisdell never came through to any real work of
distinction, although he had all kinds of promise.

Another interesting experience I had was an interview
with Boies Penrose, then United States Senator. He told
me more of the political game than I had ever heard from
anyone else. I remember the last time I saw him. He was
standing in the train shed at Powelton Avenue. He was
then United States Senator at Washington. He was carrying three bits of baggage, all himself, two big dress suit-
cases and a bag. If that wasn't America, where will you
find it? I can't remember if there were redcaps in those
days. I suppose maybe he had to carry the bags. He ruled
our Pennsylvania politics as masterfully as Matthew Stan-
ley Quay had before him. I don't know whether it could
be said of him as it was said of Quay that he never broke
a promise. I never heard of his breaking one. That, of

course, was the secret of Quay's success. He built up his machines on handing out patronage, but he always gave what he promised.

What I remember most clearly of that year at the *Record* was the night that Cleveland was elected. Old Mr. Singerley was a vehement Democrat and for the first time since the Civil War he had a chance to have his party win in the national election. Of the thirty-odd of us in the local room I think all but five were Republicans. We were young and when one is young things seem amusing that do not seem so amusing to later years. Mr. Singerley ordered our supper around from Dooner's, a famous Irish hostelry on Tenth Street between Chestnut and Market on the right-hand side just south of St. Stephen's Church. Everything was ordered in for the whole lot of us, perhaps eighteen in addition to the local-room crowd, or about fifty in all, that is everything except the terrapin which was the Dooners' most famous dish. We had, I remember, chicken salad and fried oysters and coffee galore. We were kept there all night. I can't remember now what time the viands came in, but perhaps about midnight. By that time it was sure Cleveland had won. Some of the Republicans among us went out and bought who knows where—for the stores were closed by that time—yards and yards of crepe. Mr. Singerley came up to pronounce a blessing on his hopefuls dining in the small hours. He saw the crepe on the table. He was famous for his expletives. He outdid himself on this occasion. I cannot remember the adjectives except the last one, but we were several kinds of several kinds of ungrateful whelps.

That experience on the *Record* taught me how to drive through to the end of a story. It also taught me the trick of telling the whole story in the first ten lines and then taking it up from a fresh angle after the first paragraph of ten lines and telling it all over again in detail. In an exigency when there comes a press at the final make-up at 2 A.M. most of the story can be thrown out and all of it that matters be still there in the first ten lines. That taught me directness and surety of attack and gave me a power of condensation. I am very sure that there is a nearer relation to literature in the newspaper office than in the seminar room.

As I didn't have to go to work on the *Record* until one o'clock there were often free mornings for me. I had an early lunch which was really a breakfast and left for town about twelve o'clock from Upsal Station. Sometimes I'd get up early and go off for a walk before this meal. I'd get home at one o'clock in the morning say four nights of the week and at three two nights. On the mornings after the one o'clock homecoming I sometimes had the energy to go out for walks. I learned a great deal about the Wissahickon during this period and got together the material I was to use afterward in *The Wissahickon Hills*. I was writing, of course, or trying to write. Indeed there are passages in *The Wissahickon Hills* even earlier than the 1902 the first articles included therein are dated. There were passages that were memories of these experiences of the year 1892-1893.

I was going a great deal to the Delaware Valley Ornithological Club these days. The meetings every other Thursday night were big events of my life. It was then I got to know so well Witmer Stone, and only less well De Haven and Spencer Morris and Will Baily, and the other old stand-bys of that group. Of them all only Witmer Stone came through to the promise of his youth with his two volumes of *Bird Studies at Old Cape May*. It is my opinion that he was the most important author come out of Philadelphia in my lifetime. I say this realizing that we had Dr. S. Weir Mitchell, Owen Wister, Richard Harding Davis,

and George Kelly during these years. I think there is more
that is permanent in the way of good writing in these *Bird
Studies* than in any book of these so well-known authors.

In the spring of 1893 Ellis Oberholtzer, my cousin, who
had been an editorial writer on the *Evening Telegraph,*
wished to go to Germany for study. He asked me if I would
take his place and hold it for him for the two years he
would be abroad. I determined to take the chance of there
being a place for me when he came back. My transfer to
the *Telegraph* brought about a great change, of course, in
my life. I had come to think of the city in this year of night
work as a place illumined with gaslight and electric light,
of wet streets and people pouring out of the theaters into
the rain, and of empty streets in still later hours on my
return to Germantown. On certain late nights my aunt
Theora Culbertson took me in. She lived on Saunders Avenue opposite the Presbyterian Hospital. They always killed
the fatted calf for me. I shall never forget the many good
meals I had there.

My cousins the Ellises also took me in often at night for
meals. They had a standing invitation for me to come
there every Friday night, when they had an elaborate fish
dinner. This, by the bye, was what taught me to like fish.
I had avoided it up to this time but one simply couldn't
resist the hospitality of that board with the many children
sitting around the table. In that day there were gardens
in the back yards of the places on Greene Street and I have
eaten corn grown on the place on those Friday evenings so
long ago.

What really mattered at the *Telegraph* was my introduction to the stage. Edward Schwartz was the dramatic
critic and Watson Ambruster the managing editor. Both
were deeply interested in the stage. They covered every
theater. I was broken in on the Girard Avenue Theatre

and a dozen others before I was entrusted with plays at the South Broad Street Theatre or at the Walnut Street Theatre or at the Chestnut Street Opera House or at the Chestnut Street Theatre. The Girard Avenue Theatre was in those days under the management of George Holland, and his brothers, E. M. Holland and Joseph Holland, often acted there with him. Frank Doane was the leading comedian and Amy Lee the soubrette. There were two Knowles Sisters who played first and second leads. Creston Clarke was often there as a visiting star, and Russ Whitall. I saw a great many of the Victorian "masterpieces" there. I saw *Conn the Shaughran* and other Boucicault plays. I saw old English comedy, *She Stoops to Conquer* and *The Rivals*. I saw the successes of the Daly and Frohman and Palmer companies after they were several years old.

Another theater at which I was broken in was the National Theatre, which was at Tenth Street where Ridge Avenue crosses or just south of that crossing. This was the home of melodrama. Here I have actually seen the moved spectator climb on the stage to attack the villain. Here I saw smashes of trains, head-on collisions, wrecks, tank dramas in which there were attempted suicides, heroic rescues, all under the flashing lights of night on dark water. Another house that I was sent to was the Forepaugh Family Theatre on North Eighth Street. I remember seeing there Pinero's *Amazons* played as low comedy instead of the high comedy it had been when I had seen it on Chestnut Street. The Bijou Theatre was also on North Eighth Street. There were two theaters in Kensington, although these I was seldom sent to. In the heart of the city there was the old Arch Street Theatre, once the home of the Drews, but now a theater for the Yiddish drama. It was there in the later years I was to see Orleneff in a remarkable performance of Ibsen's *Ghosts*.

The famous old Dime Museum was then at Tenth and Arch Streets. Carncross's Opera House, the home of Negro minstrelsy, was at Eleventh and Girard. I had been taken to Carncross's by Mr. Van Schaick, our next-door neighbor on Tulpehocken Street, who thought that my education was being neglected, that my folks were too highbrow to let me know what Negro minstrelsy was. On Chestnut Street there was the Chestnut Street Theatre below Thirteenth and the Chestnut Street Opera House above Tenth Street. Then came the Garrick on Chestnut Street below Broad and right around the corner on South Broad Street at Sansom was the Forrest, on the back of what had been the Dundas-Lippincott property. I remember going to see the Negro Booth at the Standard Theatre on South Street, but whether I was sent there or whether that was a slumming trip, I cannot remember. I remember going to see Italian marionettes down somewhere about Eighth and Mariott in company of an Italian sculptor who was a student at the Academy of Fine Arts.

In these days what is now the Shubert Theatre was Horticultural Hall, the place of the flower shows in that time. I saw many plays, generally very much injured by the great stage, at the Academy of Music. On North Broad Street was the Park Theatre at Broad and Fairmount Avenue. I remember I saw there for the first time Pinero's *The Profligate* with Marie Burroughs and John Kellerd, its feature the fall she made down seven steps landing on her shoulder and rolling over without injury and with extreme discretion. I think that is what made the play as far as Philadelphia was concerned, Marie Burroughs' fall. It was the second version of the play, that in which the heroine, a young wife, dashes the cup of poison from her husband's lips just as he is about to commit suicide.

Further up North Broad Street was the Grand Opera

House where I heard so many summer operas under Gustav Hinrichs' lease of the place. There were two full sets of stars of second and third magnitude. The first group had as tenor, Guille; as baritone, Guiseppe del Puente; as basso, W. H. Clarke. The soprano was Selma Koert-Kronold and the contralto was Clara Poole. The second group consisted of Payne Clark, tenor; Wilhelm Mertens, baritone; and a basso whose name I cannot recall. Dallett Fuguet's cousin Stephen afterward tried his hand at opera in the minor basso roles. The women in the second group were Greta Risley and Marie Van Cauteren. The orchestra was of about forty and included as one of the bull fiddlers a man I afterward got to know well as a waiter in a restaurant on Dock Street in my *Evening Telegraph* days. Koert was the first violin, the husband of Selma Kronold. Later Campanari, who had been a cello player in the Boston Symphony Orchestra, came to the company and created the role of Tonio in *I Pagliacci*. I shall never forget the tremendous ovation after his singing of the famous prologue, nor shall I ever forget the sardonic look of Albert Guille when at the end of that play he stuck his thumbs in the armholes of his vest and declared, said, not sang, "La comedia è finita," the comedy is finished, of course. I also heard and saw the first performance of *Cavalleria Rusticana* here earlier in this same opera house. In all I saw forty operas here, the first of which was Beethoven's *Fidelio,* with Payne Clark as Florestan and Selma Koert-Kronold as Fidelio. All this, of course, was in the days before the summer concerts of Walter Damrosch at Willow Grove did away with the vogue of the opera at Broad and Montgomery Avenue.

Another feature of my *Telegraph* experience was the writing of a series of articles on the contemporary American and English poets. I wrote, I remember, a column printed on the last column of the editorial page on Emily Dickinson, on Carl Lüders, and on Father Tabb. I remember I met Harrison Morris on Chestnut Street one day after the Lüders article and the Tabb article had appeared. He said, "How could you, after writing so good an article on Lüders, praise that good-for-nothing?"

I said, "I could write a worse article on Harrison S. Morris."

Among the English poets that I wrote about were Yeats, and Davidson, and Kipling, and William Watson, and Francis Thompson. Some of this writing was the first to recognize these men in America. I wrote to all the men before I printed articles about them and I have still some of those letters. I remember one from Davidson which said, "It is hardly fair to ask the questions you ask of a poet. However, I answer them even if I think it unreasonable for you to ask more than fruit of the apple tree. What you ask is for the tree not only to bear blossom and set fruit. You ask it to pick its own fruit, to pare, core, cook and serve that fruit on the table." He went on to do just all those things.

I shall never forget the dreadful Sabbath day I put in over Hardy's *Jude the Obscure*. It opened a winter day with a wild northeaster and all day long I read *Jude the Obscure* to the pounding of rain on the third-story roof of my father's house on Upsal Street. At nine o'clock at night I had finished the book. I couldn't stand indoors any longer and went out into the wild storm, faced it up Upsal Street to the northeast and was glad of the sting of rain in my face.

CHAPTER 10

JOE, DALLETT, AND I

THE triumvirate of Joe Head and Dallett Fuguet and I had begun back in 1892, in the seminar of Professor Schelling's class in Elizabethan drama at the University of Pennsylvania. We continued to meet and to discuss one another's attempts at verse during the early years of my newspaper experience. We had a number of trips out into the country together and we had the advantage of trying out each other's point of view. There were never three men more diametrically opposed in regard to political or social beliefs than we three. Dallett was the typical mugwump. Joe Head's folks, because some of them were from Louisiana, were old-fashioned Bourbon Democrats, but Joe had gone partway toward socialism. He carried us off to meetings of Eugene Debs. I could not listen very carefully to Debs as he spoke because I was fascinated by his foot play. He spoke, the Socialist, in evening clothes. He stood in the middle of the stage with his two feet pressed close together as we used to have to press them in my earliest days at the Germantown Academy when we rose to greet Mrs. Kershaw. His arms gesticulated like a gently turning windmill. When he wished to move about, instead of stepping around, he worked himself sideways with those two feet still tightly pressed together. Of course what he had to do was to move from a position directly facing the audience to a position forty-five degrees right or left. Then throwing his heels around again he would bring himself to a position directly fronting the audience. In this fashion he gravitated from one side of the stage to the other. I was so sure that he was going to trip over his own feet that I couldn't listen to his arguments.

Later on when Joe became prosperous he ceased to be socialistic. I haven't seen much of him in recent years. In fact, I saw very little of him after Dallett's death in 1935. After the death of Dallett's wife, Nell, and the marriage of his children, Dallett moved into a little room somewhere in the heart of New York. He had no space even for his books. He sent me some of them. Dallett was one of the grave and quiet Spaniards. His reddish beard perhaps spoke some Teutonic blood, but he was the sort that would rather watch and listen than talk. He missed nothing. He had a keen sense of humor and a rather wicked pen. He was hardly quick enough in talk, although there, too, he got in a good thrust now and then.

I learned a good deal through him. After he left Philadelphia he established himself in a half hall room at No. 53 West Ninth Street in a rooming house in which were Arthur Stedman and a fellow named Hyde who did a good deal of reviewing for *The Bookman*. That place and the adjoining French restaurant to which Dallett took me now and then were as close to Bohemia as I ever got. I remember that one time I was there with Dallett we went to this restaurant for breakfast. The rolls were famous, the coffee was famous, but it was only one roll and one cup of coffee that I could enjoy. In my sentimental youth the sight of a big, black, bouncing Negro coming into the room and being greeted by a white French wife with open arms spoiled my breakfast. She was a stunning-looking person. We had hardly been able to understand the children that were with her. We understood after her black husband came in. They were tawnies. I suppose these were West Indians from Haiti.

The only other coast of Bohemia I ever neared was

through my cousin Jesse Godley. He died in 1888. I inherited his three ducks. He had lived down at Secane after having married an artist named Winifred Fay. She and Jesse were both members of a group gathered about Frank Stevens. Frank conceived the idea of a brotherhood of artists because he had been reading William Morris. He designed to lead a sort of pre-Raphaelite brotherhood in little in Philadelphia. The group acquired a stable in a little street back of the Masonic Temple at Broad and Filbert. There I met the two Stevens' and C. C. Cooper, who was afterward to paint the canyons of the skyscraper district of New York and the line of those buildings against the sky as you saw them from the ferries at Communipauw. "Has" Morris had some affiliations with this group, but I can't remember any more of them than Cooper and the two Stevens' and Jess. Jess was a sculptor and a pretty good one. Some of the carvings around the door of the Academy of Natural Sciences on Nineteenth Street near Race are his, and there used to be one of his statues at the entrance to the Zoological Gardens.

Jess had many strange tales to tell of the zoo. One time he was modeling an elephant pegged out for a little freedom from his cage. All of a sudden he heard a trumpeting and saw the elephant make violently in his direction, pulling up the peg. Jess started off hugging his clay. Fortunately, the elephant was diverted by the umbrella under which Jess was working. He stopped and seized and demolished that as Jess sought the safety of a house near by.

I went several times with Jess to meetings these young men held in the second story of their stable. I do not suppose they talked more nonsense than most folks, young or old. However, I learned about art and life from them.

In later years Dallett was of inestimable help when from 1901 to 1907 I was editor of the graduate magazine of the

University of Pennsylvania, *The Alumni Register* as it was
called in those days. I owed this job to Sam Houston. I
was a little boy when he was a bigger boy on Tulpehocken
Street. He lived next door but one. He was very active in
Pennsylvania affairs when I returned in '97 to teach in the
English Department there. He knew I needed money and
he asked me if I didn't want to take the editorial job on
the *Register*. That meant a very great deal to me. I was
wanting to get married and that could be justified only by
what I had in reserve from my savings. I was twenty-eight
by this time in 1900 and certainly a bit more settled than
I had been at twenty-one. I was married to Sara Matlack
Roberts, a fellow Germantowner, in 1900.

I do not know how it was that little jobs of hack work
came my way. They did, however. I suppose people knew
I needed the money and turned things in my direction. I
remember making three dollars an afternoon in doing
biographies for *Universities and Their Sons, The University of Pennsylvania.* You could just dig out and write a
biography in three to four hours' work and I spent many
afternoons in the library at that. After all, if you could
pick up fifteen or eighteen dollars that way in a week, it
meant a very great deal. It meant cream with coffee.

All this time there was still to the fore my love of birds.
I was writing about them and spending hours in their ob-
servation even as I am today.

I would appeal to Dallett when the University gave an
LL.D. to John Singer Sargent or a Litt.D. to James Whit-
comb Riley. Dallett was well read in American literature
as in English. He was interested in a come-outer photographic magazine that was inspired by Stieglitz, one of the
first men who thought that an artist could express himself
through the photographic plate as freely as with brush and
color. Dallett knew about painting. Dallett had good taste

in all departments of art. I remember his taking us to a
performance of *Lohengrin* when we went over to visit him
at Montclair. I remember trips with him across Green-
wood Lake and up the mountain at its head and the buying of the most redoubtable peach brandy I ever met in
my life, peach brandy that had been made by the fourth
generation of a family to whom the copper worm had descended. There was also for sale at the hostelry on the
heights fox skins of a brilliant red. It has been my luck to
have most of the foxes I have met rather faded out or
tawny and not of the brilliant red that those skins, un-
doubtedly December skins, had taken on.

Sara and I went to Dallett's at Durham, Connecticut, on
our wedding trip. I shall always remember our visit there.
Old Mr. Coe, Nell's grandfather, had been a steamboat
engineer on the Mississippi. He had been everything else,
too, I think. He said to me when we were going up to bed,
"Just put your shoes out and the man will take care of
them." I had seen no man. All I had seen was a most big-
bodied and bony-shouldered Finn maid, a woman that
looked as if she could kill an ox with one blow. I had seen
no man. I thought perhaps somebody came in to do the
chores. I put the shoes out. Next morning there they were,
beautifully polished.

Said Mr. Coe at breakfast, "How did you like the shine
the man gave your shoes?"

I said, "Such a shine is surely worth a quarter."

The old man held out his hand and declared in high
glee, "I shined them. I learned that on the steamboats on
the Mississippi." He did not take the quarter.

I put some of my own stuff into the *Register,* but not a
very great deal of it. While I was on the *Evening Telegraph* I had written an editorial entitled "Pennsylvanisch
Deitsch." We had more letters about that than we had for

any other editorial that winter. Only a hair tonic on the women's page brought forth more letters. I furbished up this old editorial and worked into it a review of a book about the Kloster at Ephrata, *Brother Jabez*. That was the beginning of my writing about things Pennsylvania Dutch. I had been brought up, of course, on innumerable stories of Father's trips to Easton as a boy. Father was very much interested in his people and had preserved a number of memorials. After his death I found a box full of these things.

I also put in an article on Yeats. Percy Moore, of the School of Biology, and Edwin Brumbaugh, then an undergraduate, Martin's son, the architect of today, and I got up an article on the birds of the campus. That, too, went in. Altogether we had listed sixty-seven, I think it was. I remember to this day a performance of *Midsummer Night's Dream* over in the Botanical Gardens that was attended with morrums, morrums, morrums from the bullfrogs in the pond, and by a song of a wood robin there in Woodlands Cemetery close by the old Hamilton house. One winter there were a pair of Cooper's hawks on the tower at the east end of College Hall. They used to drop down just outside my window and snitch sparrows out of the ampelopsis with their feet. Once Pomp, the college janitor, brought me "two buds puffed up same as toads." They were young night hawks which had been found back of a chimney on the roof. I have seen a yellow palm warbler come out of the ventilating radiator in the wall of Room 213, and I have been brought chimney swifts that had got into rooms by that same involved entranceway.

In 1901 we went to Nova Scotia for an outing. We went across from Boston to Yarmouth on a wild night in an undermanned ship with no discipline at all. We had tickets to Halifax but we went as far north only as Wolfville. The whole country was aflame between Wolfville and Halifax. The valley of the Gaspareau made more of an impression upon me as an apple country than as the background of the Evangeline story. It was here I first saw apple trees being really taken care of. In that primitive time there were people scrubbing scale off the limbs of trees with scrubbing brushes. They were sending apples by schooner from Wolfville to England.

On our return south we stopped at Smith's Cove. We stayed at a boardinghouse run by a Canuck. He had been a ship's cook. Here we met one of the first pickers of antiques I had ever run across. She showed us two Crown Derby cups and saucers she had got from a tar-paper-covered shack up the mountain back of Smith's Cove from a connection of Martin Farquhar Tupper, the poet of *Proverbial Philosophy*. Here, too, we met an old man who had built an eyrie in a tree from which an Englishman could shoot a moose. The old fellow had been salting the moose there and had it nice and tame even when we were there. He said the Englishman couldn't help but hit it if he could shoot at all.

It was here one day we were surrounded by a group of young cattle that almost knocked us down. They were crazy for salt. They nosed into us and insisted on licking our hands and tried to lick our faces. It was a rather upsetting experience. All we could do was to edge away backward from them until we got to a fence, and then escape. We escaped I suppose because after all most of them were young creatures, some of them hardly more than well-grown calves and none of them more than yearlings.

It was here, too, an old man had been building his tomb, a concrete tomb on the end of which some godless American had painted an American flag, much to the distress of the good Nova Scotian who swore by the Union Jack.

When he was sixty-eight and still at sea as a captain he had a vision in which it was revealed to him that he would die when he was seventy. As soon as he was ashore from this trip he began building his mausoleum. He built it of concrete with just two niches in it, one for himself and one for his wife. He was seventy-eight when we were there and he had been enlarging his tomb to give himself something to do when he didn't die as the vision said he would at seventy. It was this story I told one day in class with results.

Perhaps a year later a boy came to me and planked down $7.50 on the table in 213. I said, "What's this?"

He said, "This is your half of the pay I got for writing up that story of the mausoleum in Nova Scotia you told us in class in the Blank Bank Magazine. I told Father about it and he said I hadn't any business to take information I had got in class and sell it, that just as the letter written belongs to the writer of the letter so the story told in the classroom belongs to the teller of the story. However," the boy said, "I didn't agree with father and I thought the best compromise for me would be to give you half of the fifteen dollars I got for the story."

I explained to him carefully that there was such a thing as classroom privilege, that it was one with club privilege, that what was said in the classroom should not be repeated save with permission outside of the classroom, that is, anything of an intimate nature. Of course, I refused the $7.50, but I couldn't persuade this man that his action was not according to Hoyle. This boy, of course, was in college on a scholarship, and his thought was that his tuition was paid for and therefore he had a right to use all that came to him in that tuition. This was the youth who found the girl to whom he was engaged could not talk to him about all his literary likes. She had gone to a college that set its face sternly against the consideration of any living authors. He therefore came to me and asked me if this girl could take my graduate class as a hearer although she had been only two years at college. I said, "Of course." He said he would come and get her at the end of the hour. This left her a certain amount of freedom. I diagnosed the case correctly and said to her: "It is all right with me if you just turn up at class in time to go home with Mr. Blank." She heaved a deep sigh of relief, gave me a ravishing glance, and acquiesced.

It was at Smith's Cove also that I was told a very strange story of long, long ago by an old man picking up apples. He said, "They are good to me. My son's wife is good to me, but," he said, "I don't like the cider she makes. She puts no sweet apples in the cider. There ought always be a touch of sweet apple juice in cider for cider to be right." He was bent double. He crept along with a cane like an old man on the stage, in the three-legged phase of development. He had on an old cardigan jacket which had faded from its original brown to a kind of greeny yellow. He looked up at you with a kind of turtle's glance from under his hat out of rheumy eyes that watered and had very small and very pale blue irises. He said, "Maybe I'm not like world's folks. Perhaps I was born a bit queer." He said, "You know, it was this way. When my mother was carrying me, my father was at sea. She was left home with just herself in the house and her sister living close by, but she was alone in the house and she was expecting me. Word came that Father had been drowned in a storm at sea. She got the horse and sleigh and got a neighbor man to take down one of those iron cradles in which they used to burn pine knots as beacons, and fastened it on the end of the sleigh. She did that because she knew the wolves were very bad between Smith's Cove here and Annapolis and down on the other side of Annapolis Basin.

"Well, she started out with that cradle fastened to the end of the sleigh with the burning pine knots. She started out at night to drive forty miles over the snow to bring back Father's body. When she got around there to where it was, after all kinds of trouble, and having to pretty near fight the wolves off despite the burning brands, she saw a great pile of what she thought was cordwood. It wasn't cordwood. It was the bodies of all the men had been drowned and washed up by the sea. They were all frozen stiff so they piled them up same as cordwood and built big fires round about them so the wolves shouldn't get to them. It was some job sorting out the body of her man. Mind you, she was carrying me all the time and might have easily brought on a miscarriage. She stuck at it and found Father. She put him on the sleigh. She got a new supply of pine knots and she drove home safe with Father followed by wolves and wolves and wolves.

"Well, you know when you have been born of a woman that had a heart like that maybe you are not just like the neighbor in the house down the road that's too lazy to build a chimney four feet above the shingles, and so burns his house down."

We went across from Digby to St. John in New Brunswick and then went up to Frederickton. Here we found an old hotel entirely furnished with Empire furniture, mahogany. On our way down St. John River from Frederickton to St. John we had many water stops. At one of them I remember a man in the full canonicals of the Episcopal Church putting aboard the carcass of a steer. I'll always remember him standing up in the boat with that creature on his shoulder and passing it to men who had opened a gangway in the side of the ship.

We were fed fresh salmon on that boat from Frederickton to St. John. It was the best I ever ate. On the way back to Boston by boat from St. John it was foggy all the way until we were off Portland. We saw very little of Grand Manan and other places I very much wished to see. One of the memories of Smith's Cove that I forgot to state when I was referring to it was the ravens. They flew over in the air too high for us to see the ruff of feathers on their breasts but not too high for their clarion notes to fall to us out in the still of evening.

CHAPTER 11

COLLEGE COURSES

I HELD a reader's job and did graduate work at Pennsylvania in the college year 1891-1892, the year after my graduation. The graduate work so disheartened me I fled to newspaper work. As an undergraduate I had had the best of all the courses; now I had, as one of my teachers owned, the skim milk along with the cream. So it is with most students not born gerund grinders. It is in the second year of graduate work, when they have found their way to a thesis subject of their own, and begin to realize that fields of study seemingly remote from human interest have a relation to their own individual research, that they widen horizons and give balance, it is then and only then that nine out of ten graduate students can look forward happily on the long road to the Ph.D.

I was glad to get back to college teaching after those five years of newspaper work, 1892-1897. It was hard sledding the first year of teaching, for they gave me four courses to work up with only four months' preparation before the courses began. In the fall of 1897 I taught English composition to freshmen and sophomores, both required courses, and two required courses in sophomore literature, one on the English novel from Fielding to George Eliot, and one on the nineteenth-century essay, from Lamb to Stevenson.

I had always worked hard, at chores about the place and in watching birds and beasts and, in recording my observations of them, at school and college studies I liked. I read very rapidly, more rapidly than anyone I ever met save my colleague Clarence Child, who can take in every word on a page while I am taking in two-thirds of it. I had been an omnivorous reader from the age of four, at which I began to read. I had read, I repeat, all of Scott before I went to college, and in college I had read Fielding and Smollett and Sterne, but I had bogged down in Richardson. I had read about half of Dickens and about half of Thackeray, but only *Silas Marner* and *Adam Bede* and *The Mill on the Floss* of George Eliot. All the novelists were in Father's library, and, as I was living at home, they were readily accessible to me. Still, I had to work morning, noon, and night to keep ahead of my classes.

I was strong and energetic. I had had one very serious illness, typhoid fever, when I was working on the *Evening Telegraph*. I so nearly died I was interesting to doctors. I was written up as a case, "Mr. X of Germantown." However, I recovered quickly and was my old self again two years later when I took up work at Pennsylvania. Though there had been teachers in my family before me I was none too sure I could teach. I knew I could by the spring of 1898, but I suffered tortures of uncertainty during the fall of 1897. Clarence Child, who all the years since has given me aid and comfort and good counsel, told me that "the first year of teaching is hell." It was. I had no time to do what I would, no time off all winter. So it was for years afterward. My nose was to the grindstone for thirty years. I stood it because my heart was in the work, because it turned out that I could teach. Some of my newspaper writing had been the first middlemanning of contemporary English poets to America, and that middlemanning was continued by my college teaching.

As early as the catalogue of 1898-1899 I am listed for "Contemporary Poetry," English 17, one hour a week. By 1902, 17 became 255, two hours a week. English 246, "Nineteenth-Century Drama," is listed in 1904, but it was not given, I think, until 1905. I had been advanced to the rank of assistant professor in 1904, and in 1907 I was further advanced to a professorship of English literture. In 1911-12 I began giving "English Literature in Ireland." That was the winter of the first visit of the Abbey Players to America, and of the riot over *The Playboy of the Western World* of Synge at Broad and Cherry Streets in Philadelphia.

I first gave "The Contemporary Novel" in 1913-1914 to the undergraduates. It had been given the year before in the Graduate School. There I had begun graduate teaching in 1907 with "Contemporary Poetry" and "The Contemporary Drama." "English Literature in Ireland" was added in the Graduate School in 1909. These four courses, virtually a consideration of all English literature save the essay, from 1850 on, were my chief concern in teaching for a quarter of a century, with "Contemporary Drama" with the undergraduates the most popular of the four courses. It was not the one that I liked best, that was "Contemporary Poetry." As I said in the preface to *Tuesdays at Ten* (1928), poetry has always been to me the touchstone to all literature. If there is not poetry, the quality of poetry, lyricism, in prose play or prose novel or prose essay, it is not great literature to me.

In 1929-1930 I gave for the first time English 108, a course in the contemporary essay. It is concerned with such writers as Max Beerbohm, Samuel Butler, G. K. Chesterton, Doughty, Norman Douglas, Gissing, Cunninghame-Graham, W. H. Hudson, Alice Meynell, Arthur Symons, and Edward Thomas. I am not sure whether this was a road-breaking course, as that in the drama from Bulwer to Barrie had been, and that in contemporary poetry from Henley to Kipling, and eventually to Blunden and Auden, and as that in "The Celtic Renaissance" or "English Literature in Ireland" had been. "The Contemporary Novel" was but a carrying on, through another generation of writers, of the course in the novel Felix E. Schelling had given for the first time in any American university back in the late 1880's.

The course in "The Contemporary Essay" is that of all courses I am most qualified to give. I can write essays. I know from the inside how they are written. I have the understanding as one of the trade what are the secrets of the trade. I cannot hold that one who would talk of poetry or drama or novel must be able to write in the forms he talks about, or that he who would talk of any one of the forms of writing must be able to write it. I know too many teachers of literature, teachers of the first power, who cannot write. I do know, however, that an ability to write helps largely in one's teaching of literature. If the man talking to a class has himself some standing in letters the classes are much more apt to take his say-so than if he cannot write.

All my middlemanning of literature has been very simple. I read all that my author has written. I digest each of his books for my lectures. I work up his biography as fully as I can. In many instances I write the author for explanation of this and that. I have had a good few of contemporary British writers to lecture at Pennsylvania. I know these men and have had long talks with them. I talk everything over with others who are interested in letters. I begin my own lectures with biography, give the dates of publication of the author's books chronologically, and then divide all Gaul into three parts. By that I mean I make one division of Yeats as (1) poet; (2) playwright; (3) essayist; (4) storyteller; (5) propagandist; etc., and then again subdivide these groups. Under Yeats as poet I make the subdivisions (a) lyric; (b) narrative; (c) dramatic; (d) gnomic. I mention this poem as illustrative of one subdivision of his work, and that of another. I take, for instance, "The Valley of the Black Pig" as illustrative of his gnomic poetry, and describe the background of Carrowmore against which it was written, and try to explain title and cryptic lines, such as, for instance, "Master of the still stars and of the flaming door." At the end of all I try to put Yeats over against such poets as have influenced him, Sir Samuel Ferguson, William Morris, Shelley, Milton, Donne, Spenser.

When I was young, lines of poetry imprinted themselves on my memory without effort on my part. I have forgotten many I once knew, but I still remember enough to illustrate Yeats as balladist, or Yeats enlarging a line of folk verse into a poem. I can recall "When I was a boy with never a crack in my heart," just as I can recall lines of good prose casually dropped in conversation. These latter, however, I write down as soon as I can, just as I get up in the middle of the night to write down a phrase that has come to me that will fit into something I am writing. In like fashion I can remember things seen fifty years ago, the cattle on the beach below Anglesea against a background of holly trees, Uncle Jim in red tights and cap and bells as he dropped in on us on his way to a fancy dress party, the look of agony in the eyes of a rabbit my chum had shot.

I use my own experience of life to test the truth of the life portrayed in play or novel. I put the clowns of Hardy against the clowns of Shakespeare, the verse of W. H. Davies against the verse of Herrick, the prose of W. H. Hudson against the prose of Izaak Walton. I think every phase of present-day literature should be seen against a background of its kind back to Chaucer "grand against the ancient morn." I stress repetition and concrete illustration, and I make several approaches to all difficult subjects, say "The Listeners" of Walter De La Mare. I read the class that poet's "Motley," trying to put into the tones of my reading the changing moods of the fool's monologue.

I quote and try to explain "the readings of life" you find in all good writing. Frost's "Nothing gold can stay," or Lamb's "The world meets nobody half way." I try to pick out characters that are "figures against the sky," a Wife of Bath, a Falstaff, a Widow Wadman, a Becky Sharp, a Tess. I compare such a moment as Michael Henchard's death on Egdon with that of Lear on the Heath, Hardy again over against Shakespeare. I make much of the distinction between theatrical effect and dramatic truth, of the transitoriness of such literature of ideas as *The Passionate Friends* of Wells and of the permanence of the literature which is loyal to life as you find it in Conrad's *Victory*. I spend a great deal of time over the phrases of critics I have found helpful, lordship of language, lyrical cry, natural magic, large accent, grand style, wise dicta from Coleridge and Arnold and Symons.

Above everything else I din it in that literature is a part of life, as necessary to every man as work and play, as sport and gossip, as food and sweat, as daily paper and fortnightly show, as symphony music and automobile outings. I have insisted for years on years that literature is a something beautiful made in words out of a man's experience or dream of life, that it is a reducing to order of some part of the chaos of life, that it is a highly selective art and not a photographic art. I hold there is still plenty to write about in the world, that fairly cries out to be written about, and without scooping the dregs of things that most authors are too good a sort to dredge up.

I am a stout believer in tradition. I believe with Robert Frost that a work of art must depend on an older work of art. Of a hundred revelations that he has made to me, or that have come to me when my mind was illuminated by his, one that recurs again and again is that a 5 to 10 per cent change in literature constitutes all the originality we can stand. A poet's poetry must necessarily be nine-tenths of what has been in the poetry before him.

I have had enough of lecturing. It has been good, but I have had enough of it, just as I have had enough of the city, of the theater, of opera, of going to football games. I am as effective at seventy-four as I ever was, though it takes more out of me to be effective now than when I was young. I have enjoyed the talk with boys in my office that is so large a part of a teacher's job, and I enjoy it still, but I have little time left now for what I wish to do before I die, and I grudge the time given to many things that have meant much to me. The reading of papers, though, is my heaviest chore. I have not the drive to get through them I once had.

I gave up graduate work in 1935, because the necessity of keeping up with the reading for my courses and the bibliography of their subjects left me no leisure for writing. My methods of teaching and my courses have traveled rather far. Old students of mine are giving my courses and following my methods of classroom talk in many parts of the country. My methods have been adopted by students in other subjects than English. A talk on botany I heard the other night revealed my way of doing things even to mannerisms. I have always talked my lectures, never just read them. I have always had to study my lesson the night before class to have that class go well.

CHAPTER 12

FRESH FIELDS AND PASTURES NEW

IN 1902 we went to Ireland. We sailed from Philadelphia on the *Nordland* and landed at Queenstown, as it was then, the port of entry for Cork. As we got off the ship there were women selling gooseberries on the quay. I had often heard of the proficiency in bad language of fishwives. I was now to hear it. It was the time of the Boer War. A Tommy came by with a hat about the size of a teacup on one side of his head and the strap from it around under his chin to hold it in place. He said to the woman with the gooseberries, "Mother, how much the gooseberries?"

"You blank blank bastard of a blankety blank blank. I'm not your mother, and you may be very sure that I wouldn't have been. I'd have no child by a man that would get the like of you." And more of the same. And more of the same. I had been told by numerous kindly Irish people that the gooseberries in Ireland were as big as English walnuts in America. It is true they were. I was waiting for the old woman to show her dexterity by driving them at the offending Tommy, but she didn't. They were, I suppose, too precious. I had been intending to buy some, but she lost the sale. I was too afraid of what she might say to me to offer to buy any of them. There was a sister to her about fifty feet down the quay and two more before we escaped. They were soliciting sales volubly and exchanging remarks in Irish as well as addressing us in English.

It was this night under our window in Cork that a man sang a ballad of 102 stanzas celebrating all of Ireland's heroes and England's enemies from Brian Boru to Cornelius De Wet, the South African leader. I counted the stanzas. I remember we had breaded filet of sole for supper in that hotel and that the lady of my heart enjoyed her first meal in eleven days.

We had met on the boat a doctor from Nantucket who had been a carpetbagger in the South after the Civil War. He was a "jiner." After the ship's doctor had got drunk and disappeared, our carpetbagger looked after the ailments of the folks on board the ship that had to be looked after. He explained to me, after I suppose he had tried many signs on me, that I evidently didn't belong to anything.

"No," I said, "I'm not a 'jiner.'"

"Well," he said, "you ought to be. Now watch yourself go through the customs and watch me go through." He had no trouble. I do not know whether he gave a grip or a high sign. I saw nothing, but none of his luggage was examined at Queenstown to see whether he had tobacco or liquor. Our luggage was gone through carefully. We had no tobacco and only a flask which was on my hip and which I was not searched to discover.

Our trip took us on Monday morning to Macroom on the way to Glengariff and Killarney. The first person we saw in Macroom was a Jewish peddler the very spit of the kind we had left on the streets at home. We took a char-à-banc at Macroom for Glengariff. There were two very voluble American maidens of five and thirty on the char-à-banc. They gave instructions to the man driving it as to the speed he should take in this place and that. Here they wished to look at something and demanded he should go slow. Here they were not interested in the scenery and demanded he should go fast. There were three boys from England also in the char-à-banc. One of them read a novel and refused to look at any scenery. After the driver could

WILLIAM B. YEATS
DUBLIN, 1902

THE PENNSYLVANIA COUNTRYSIDE

stand it no longer, I mean the talk of the two Irish-American ladies, he came back at them. One of them had just said to him, "Apparently you will pay no heed to what a lady says." This is what he thrust back over his shoulder at them, as the whip came back and almost got a militant and provocative feather from the hat of one of the ladies: "If either of you was a lady, maybe I'd know how to treat you as such. I'll show you my horsemanship in a minute by plucking a feather out of your hat with the end of the whip." They subsided for a minute, but they came back at him and swapped such passages at arms all the way to Glengariff.

We stopped for lunch at a delightful little inn at Inchageela where we had heather honey on our bread. There was excellent breast of chicken, I remember. It was a sort of cold lunch with coffee. When we took the char-à-banc again there was a priest with a red setter dog, a priest of breadth of back and length of back and breadth of beam. He said to me looking about at me, "Do you see the way the dog is looking at yon bush?"

I said, "I do."

He said, "It's a bush maybe that would be fairy haunted. The dogs, you know, are knowledgeable beasts. This one I have has the second sight." If there had not been too many people about I would have learned more of his appreciation of the other people. He evidently cared for them as well as believed in their existence. He thought they should be considered.

As we went up toward Keimenaigh Pass we stopped off at some kind of religious house of old time where we met a man could speak no English. He was a shepherd in a white felt cloak carrying a long staff. It wasn't a crook for it had no bend at the end. Down in the Pass we saw for the first time the dipper. We saw the little bird walk down to the stream and then disappear under its waves. It came out on the other side.

That night at Glengariff we saw a man picking peas off a stepladder. I had been brought up on many stories as to the height of the vines grown in Ireland, but even Laurence Kelly had never told me that they grew so high that a man had to have a ladder to be picking them. It was here at Glengariff we met an old body deeply concerned with our drinking of ice water. "Eh, sure it is you'll be up in the middle of the night and seeking the doctor after that," she told us. The waiters there were Germans, spies I suppose, for the First World War even in 1902 was being prepared for by Germany.

From Glengariff we went to Killarney. There the hotel was beautifully situated on the lake, but rather poor. We drove around the countryside seeing Muckross Abbey and MacGillicuddy Reeks. Muckross Abbey was beautiful. It was now the property of Lord Ardilaun, erstwhile Magginis of brown stout fame. By the bye, I do not know what we would have done in Ireland without Magginis's brown stout. The three staple vegetables we had were cabbage, turnips, and potatoes. The meat we met most commonly was mutton and it was not very good. The desserts were two: plum tart, which meant plums stewed with very little sugar and covered over with a crust, no crust on the sides or underneath the fruit; the other was a sort of gelatin which had been so liberally supplied with its jellying element that it was as difficult to cut as a piece of India rubber. In fact, if you inadvertently dropped a bit of this gelatin it bounced around as livelily as a ball with which one would play jackstones.

Everywhere in the better hotels we met the German waiters. The poorer hotels, and we had some experience of them, were pretty dreadful. There was always an insufficiency of bedclothing, and very often the food was endurable and no more.

We moved on from Killarney to Limerick, staying overnight at Killaloe. Here, late as it was, there were still salmon jumping the falls. There was a stone-roofed little church in a graveyard with exposed bones just to the west of the river. We stayed at the hotel on the right bank and there I left my watch under the pillow. This necessitated our return to the place in hope of finding it, and wonder of wonders, the woman of the house had it for us. It was just above Killaloe that there came a smooth reach of the Shannon that had a round tower and the ruins of a religious house on the left and on the right a landing that led back to Lissoy, Goldsmith's deserted village that was "remote, unfriendly, melancholy, slow." This return to Killaloe brought us late to Gort, from which we were to have visited Yeats at Lady Gregory's at Coole Park. Two women on the train told us there was no place we could stay at Gort, that we would have to go on to Ardrahan. However, we tried the inn at Gort. It was nine o'clock at night and getting dusk when we knocked at the door. The woman said, "We have no rooms for you; the house is full," and shut the door in my face. However, I beat upon it lustily again and said she must take us in, that we couldn't go on. She said, "I can't do that. We are filled up. The thing for you to do is to go to Ardrahan." She told us she would dig out a boy and a jaunting car. We had with us the faithful steamer rug that we had for years after and which we finally lost at the Pettibone Tavern in Simsbury, Connecticut, after it had served us more than thirty years.

It was raining heavily by the time we got under way in the jaunting car. There were fifteen miles between us and Ardrahan. We passed Lady Gregory's domain on the left shortly after leaving Gort and a little further on on the right we saw the tall wall of Tullira Castle, the seat of Edward Martyn. Standing up on the seat of the jaunting car in a pause in the rain we could just look over and see the modern house with its old tower at the corner. When we got to Ardrahan the inn was shut. However, by beating on the door we got up a kindly maid who said, "Oh, sure, we'll take you in and give you supper." She got up a sleepy boy and made him light the kitchen fire. We had to wait half an hour, but we had a fair enough high tea, with fried eggs and cold mutton and bread and butter and tea. Fortunately, since it was not the time of any court being held or any of the country meets, there wasn't much excitement at Ardrahan and the girl was glad of so little a diversion as two Americans.

We had breakfast next morning and then drove over to Coole, turning back at least ten miles on our trail of the night before. Everything had been A 1 at Ardrahan. Apparently there was no other place in the neighborhood where folks who wanted things right could be housed.

At Coole when we were ushered into Lady Gregory's house we found Yeats reading Spenser, the great Irish poet of today reading the great English poet who visited Ireland in the late sixteenth century and was sheriff of Cork and lived in Kilcolman Castle. Yeats took us for a walk by the lake at Coole, where we saw the famous wild swans. All the thorn bushes around about the lake and all the shrubbery of every sort were blown eastward by the great gales that came in from the Atlantic less than ten miles away. There we saw "the seven woods" that were to give title to another volume of Yeats, and there he read us many of the verses that were to go into that. He read us also the prose play *Where There Is Nothing There Is God.* They had a full house, but they were cordial enough, asking us to come back after the Galway races were over a fortnight from then and spend several days at Coole. Of course, we could not go back.

We moved on to Galway for that night, where we found the town mad over the races. Never have I seen anywhere as many drunks as I saw on the streets of Galway. We got out of town just as quickly as we could and went on by char-à-banc by way of Renvyle and Killery Fjord to Westport. We passed the night at Leenane, being sent out from the hotel to a house in the neighborhood. The food everywhere was very poor. Killery Fjord was a long arm of the sea reaching far inland, a wild lonesome place. From Westport we went out to the island of Achill. There we stayed at the Richards Inn. Richards had been once to America collecting birds. He had shot American birds all the way from Camden, New Jersey, to the Delaware Water Gap. He had intended always to write a book about these birds, but he never had, nor had he written the book that he intended to write about Achill.

Richards was very talkative. He said, "You'd be Americans." We said we were. He said, "It is only the best of Americans find their way so far into the west as this. I wonder now would you be knowing the last American that mattered that was here. His name was William T. Richards and he was a marine painter."

I allowed my better half to answer. "Oh," she said, "I happen to know him. He is my uncle." Richards had not only made illustrations for the book that this fellow of the same name never wrote, but he had sent plates of his own paintings of the neighborhood for reproduction in the book, copper plates.

There was a great deal that was interesting here. My check from Pennsylvania reached me here. This was a revelation to Mr. Audrey, who had been rather snippy on an expedition the day before about the identification of a fern. He had nearly snapped Sara's head off when she had asked was "this this." "No, it is not," he said, "it is 'that that.'" She had thought it was the royal fern, but it was not. It was some other asplenium. The envelope with "The University of Pennsylvania" on the corner brought in gave us an entirely different standing in Mr. Audrey's eyes. He was a teacher in some boys' school in the west of England. He became cordiality itself and asked us to visit him at the school. We did not.

We went off on another expedition our third day on Achill, taking along cold boiled lobster for lunch. The Irish lobster as we saw him is not particularly large, a six- or seven-inch fellow, and with the best of chewing he is difficult to reduce to a digestible condition. You can kind of feel the pieces of him scrambling about inside of you after you have partaken of him. It rained. Everybody got nice and wet. The ponies that the womenfolk rode got balky. At length there were loud complaints raised and demands of "Let us go home." Richards gave me the crooked finger. "You will never get home without a wee sup." He produced a flask and as we lay down to lap the water from the spring we also had a wee nippy to help digest the irreconcilable lobster. We made for home from the high top of the Meenawn cliffs, stopping at a lone tavern at a crossroads in the midst of a bog. Here we all went in for a sup of tea. Again came the crooked finger and I was summoned along with an Irishman returned from South Africa, a Captain Nugent, and Audrey into the back room. Here was a view of a lady unencumbered with clothes and as seductive as the houris of the worst back room in a New York bar you ever found your way into. Evidently this tavern was run by a returned Yank. They do not like the returned Yank, by the bye, in Ireland.

We got back to our inn eventually. That night as we were sitting around the fire, quite a circle of us, someone went to the piano and began going over a book of old Irish airs. A great strap of a girl with arms that reached to her knees began to sing. She was only seventeen or eighteen, but she had already appeared with the Carl Rosa Opera Company. She was a contralto, a real contralto. In the pauses between one song and another her mother leaned over to me and said, "I see by the register you are from Germantown, Philadelphia. Is the old Coulter house still standing? I spent a winter there when my husband—his name was Barlow—was a steamship ticket agent in Philadelphia." The Coulter house I have known always. It is at the corner of Main and Coulter Streets to the southeast of the Friends School and meetinghouse.

Two little priests, one an Englishman and the other an Irishman, were sitting just to my left. In a pause in the singing the little English priest got up and sang "My Love, My Queen," a most sentimental, not to say passionate, love lyric. Said the Irish priest, "Why didn't I put my hand on him and stop him from that?" as he edged over into the chair next to me. "Sure, the boy never sang that since he was a boy. I remember him singing that when we were students together at Duoay."

"That's a fine lump of a girl that's singing the contralto there," said the little priest. "I went down this morning to the wharf and what did I see but this same girl slipping out of a mackintosh, and she with very little on, and taking a head dive into the cold water way off the pier, scattering the seals and scaring the poor creatures to death the same as if they had been Christians. Ah, she could swim like a seal itself. The old men that were sitting on the pier when she made that plunge, everyone turned sideways and let a long spit out of him, and said, 'My God, she'll drown surely.' She didn't. She disturbed many a chew from one side of the cheek to the other by those old boys. You know, there is not one of them can swim because they are brought up not to swim. If they are thrown out of a boat or the boat goes down they say the water's so cold they couldn't swim far anyhow, so they have been taught not to swim because to swim would make the dying harder."

Offshore was one of the islands on which a man still lorded it over his fellows. He was known as the king of the islands. Richards had done a sketch of him for the innkeeper.

Mine host was very full of talk. He said, "Isn't it strange now my wife should be an Englishwoman? Well, this is the way she got me. I was the correspondent of an ornithological journal. You know we have golden eagles nesting on the cliffs here and I sent a paper on the golden eagle to this ornithological journal and its editor took it and published it and paid me a little for it. After I had sent him maybe a dozen other communications, what did he do but die. There came a letter from his daughter, saying, 'My father's dead and hasn't left a cent of money, and what in the world shall I do?' She had been his amanuensis in our correspondence, so I knew something of her. Well, what could an Irish gentleman do under the circumstances but write to her and say, 'Come on, my dear, over here and marry me.' She came. She married me. She has never been off the island since."

She was a very pretty woman who had borne him several children almost in her middle years. She had a wonderful head of snow-white hair and a complexion like a child's, with a girl's bloom on her cheeks. She presided at the table with absolute equanimity, although there were two Cornish choughs had the run of the room. They'd come in and light on the table and try to take the fish off you.

You had to give them the elbow. If you gave them the back of your hand, they'd give you a peck, so there was nothing to do but give them an elbow. Said the lady, "If the birds bother you, just give them the elbow and they'll take off." After the meal they came in and flew off with the bones we left on the plates. The house was clean, although not neat. The woman wondered about the future of her children. Her husband was known in the neighborhood rather unfavorably as a man who had changed from Catholic to Protestant. He was called a souper—in other words, a man who has changed his religion to get better food.

This night was the night of the coronation of Edward VII. There were watch fires on many islands and by the coast-guard huts. There wasn't too much anti-English demonstration in the neighborhood.

I was taken by Richards to see a famous shannachie, the man who had given "The King of Russia's Son" to William Larminie for his West Irish folk tales. Unfortunately he was out.

We left of a Monday morning accompanied by the two little priests. They traveled first class, we third. They said good-by to us when they got out to change for Dublin and we were going on to Sligo on the train. They were pleasant little fellows. One year they went together on a trip chosen by the English priest, the next year they came to Ireland on a trip planned by the Irish priest. This, of course, had been the Irish year. I do not know why, but I have always thought of the English priest as Father Strafford. That, as I remember it, was the name of the hero of one of Anthony Hope's stories.

At Sligo we hunted up the various spots that Yeats had written about. We went over south of the bay to see Knocknarea. This is a great pile of stones, perhaps forty feet high, on the top of which there once stood a fortified house. The pile of stones is known as Queen Maeve's Cairn. It once, of course, had had a wood stockade, with a ceiling lime washed, and had made itself a beacon that could be seen far to sea in those old times of the Vikings and their descents upon Ireland. Before we climbed Knocknarea we went into a shop in the little village to see if we could get something to fortify us for the journey. All we could buy was a two-pound piece of plum cake. It was brought forth from its place of refuge on a compote and under a bell glass cover. It was a bit hard. I saw its fellow thrown on the stage nine years afterward at the row of January, 1912, over *The Playboy* at Broad and Cherry in Philadelphia. As we left I thought it was worth while to say to the woman in the shop, "Do you know where the Yeatses lived around here?"

She said, "The Yeatses? Would it be Willie or Jack you would be meaning?" We said either. "Oh," she said, "they are everywhere. Their grandsire was the clergyman over at the Rosses on the other side of the bay. It is over around Drumcliff and the Rosses you'd better be inquiring for them, but everybody knows them around here, the Yeatses and the Pollexfens."

Years afterward when Yeats came to Philadelphia I was to find how true this was. The two maids at my aunt Sophia Godley's were from Sligo out toward Ard-na-Righ, megalithic stone monuments on the hill above Innisfree. They had Yeats "placed."

We saw the famous white stone of Ben Bulben that opens at night and allows the fairies to strike out from the underground land it is the opening to. We went out to Ard-na-Righ where there was a lamentable crying of lapwings and a lonely curlew came by as night was coming down over the bare fields.

The next day on our way back toward Dublin a girl got into our third-class compartment at a place somewhere between Sligo and Boyle. She had bade farewell to six sisters that went down in steps hardly more than a year apart. They were all crying vociferously at parting from big sister. She was dry eyed. I suppose it was not only that they were losing big sister but she was going to Dublin and they were staying at home in the little village. At Boyle the door of our compartment opened and a burly boy stumbled in and down on the seat alongside of the lady who had joined us a few miles back. She edged over toward us. A second boy threw himself in and hit the boy who was next to the lady. That boy was thrown hard against the lady and the lady catapulted over me and into the lap of Mrs. Weygandt. Turning around to Mrs. Weygandt, she said very demurely, "Sitting familiar rather than adjacent. I beg your pardon." I was delegated, of course, to move over and protect the two womenkind from the bibulous boys. Her next lead was, "You'd be Americans." We said yes. "And what are you doing in this God-forsaken corner of the world?"

"We are going up to Dublin to see if we can see anything of the Irish players."

She heaved a deep sigh and said, "I haven't had him for six weeks, but I guess you will have to have him tonight." She went on to explain that she was one Miss Gillespie and that he was Mr. James H. Cousins (Sheemus O'Cuisin), the author of *The Racing Lug* and other plays and of verses galore.

That evening he turned up at our hotel in Dublin and took us around to a rehearsal of two of his plays and of George Russell's *Deirdre* in a hall back of a produce shop. It was Pat Colum came to the door carrying a property spear and wearing a pea jacket. It was Marie Quinn who on our reaching the little hall with its plain benches said, "Now, would this be the man from Philadelphia whose last letter I didn't answer? I am Marie Quinn, the secretary of the Daughters of Erinn Association, and here's the letter I never wrote you. I have it clear in the back of my head." She is now Mrs. Dudley Digges. We met Dudley a few minutes later. Æ was there and a number of young actors who were afterward to be taken over by the Abbey Theatre Company, the brothers Fay, Marie MacShuilagh (Walker), and others.

The next day, Sunday, we went to an exhibition of the water colors of Jack Yeats and in the evening to the house of George W. Russell in the suburbs. It was a typical Philadelphia six-room house built of red brick by a returned American from Fishtown, Philadelphia. As we went in who was sitting at the door of the next place but George Moore, and who was painting him but old Jack Yeats, a portrait of the great novelist for an American admirer, John Quinn, of New York City. This was Maude Gonne's house cheek by jowl with that of George Russell. Maude we didn't see, only old Jack and George Moore, and we had only a flitting glance of old Jack and George Moore. However, I got that impression of George Moore that I carry with me still. He was built like one of those little figures that you can not turn over, that are so heavy in their posteriors that no matter what way you put them down they come to a sitting posture. He had real eighteenth-century sloping shoulders and a seedy tobacco-stained lugubrious mustache not so walrus-like as Douglas Hyde's but incipiently walrus-like.

From Dublin we went over to Holyhead and on to Liverpool and on to the Lake Country. At Windermere we found good food again. I shall never forget the clear green turtle soup at that hotel after three weeks of penitential food in Ireland. The cuisine at Windermere was most grateful. We hurried on, however, to Rydal, where it was the eve of the sports. They were to have singlestick, wrestling, and all the traditional contests. They put up a bed for us in the downstairs reception room with a French window opening on the lawn. A wagtail walked in early the next morning and paraded the room. It was almost tame.

This country was as I had always dreamed it would be. It was what William Watson describes it to be. It was a country that had the gift of rest, the gift of peace. Wordsworth's tomb by the streamside was just as you would have it. We went up, of course, to Rydal Mount and to the Dove cottage at Grasmere and found everything just as you would like it to be as Wordsworth's country. The next day as we drove over Dunmail Rise we ran into a cavalcade of all kinds of people coming into Rydal for the sports. There were donkey carriages, and goat carts, and push-carts, and wheelbarrows, and phaetons, and scores and scores and scores of folks afoot. I should have said that as we came out of our inn to take the coach that was to take us to Keswick, who should get down from that coach but William Watson. We had noticed letters stuck in a wire rack in the hall addressed to "William Watson, Esq.," but I hadn't been at all sure it would be the poet they were addressed to. However, there was no mistaking him. He had the lantern jaw, the recessed mouth, the flowing mustachios, the aloof air that one had become familiar with in the pictures of the poet. He had also what I had never bargained for, the thinnest legs I have ever beheld on any human being with the exception of the girl that lived next door but one to us on Wissahickon Avenue, whose legs were broomsticks absolutely and no more.

From there we went on to Scotland, running through

Burns's country and on to Glasgow, where we had a pig put in the bed that was to warm it that cold and rainy Saturday night. A pig is an earthenware container for hot water, the Scotch equivalent of a warming pan. Never until I had visited the hour of the unyoking of men at Paterson, New Jersey, with Dallett Fuguet, was I to meet again such a revelation of the dregs of humanity as we saw that Saturday night in Glasgow. We had driven on our way to the boardinghouse through some of the worst slums I had ever seen. Later in Los Angeles in California in 1923 I was to see as many narrow-foreheaded lowbrows.

From Edinburgh we went up to the Trossachs, by Loch Lomond with its memory of Wordsworth and "old, unhappy far off things and battles long ago"; and then to Dollar. Here we had a letter of introduction to a lady who took paying guests. We drove out on a Saturday afternoon in a blue chariot, the only equipage left in Dollar. I had not known what a Scotch town was like on a Saturday afternoon, that is a Scotch town in a coal-pit neighborhood. A burn ran down the main street of Dollar and the little houses with picturesque dooryards full of flowers fronted on the tumbling waters. Everybody in Dollar was out, however, on this Saturday afternoon, except one man in the livery stable. It took a good deal of persuasion and tippings of half crowns before we drove off in the blue chariot with a pair of spavined beasts. It was perhaps two miles out to our destination. I knocked at the door. It was opened a crack. I had the instinct to put my foot in the crack. That was something my newspaper experience had done for me. No, the lady couldn't take us in. She was leaving for Brighton on Monday morning, or Tuesday, or Wednesday at the latest. I argued and blarneyed and blustered and soon I heard the voice of an ally coming from somewhere back in the hallway. "Oh, Auntie, let us take them in." It was her niece. She had been having experiences and she wanted a little diversion.

Finally, the old lady said the real reason she couldn't take us in was that she had no maid and no food in the house. She looked at me meaningfully, although then I was slenderness itself compared to what I am now. She said, "If we do take you in, you will have to be going up to Dollar for food." It was now twilight, along between eight and nine.

"Oh, that's nothing at all," said the niece, "the three of us will walk uptown and buy minced collops." A minced collop, I should say, is a hamburg of tough lamb.

We walked up to Dollar. Already the young woman and Mrs. Weygandt had been in close conclave. I was hooshed on ahead to be out of hearing. There was intimate talk between the womenkind. Afterward, of course, I was told all that had been said, or at least as much as was necessary for a man to be told.

A man was playing bagpipes up by Castle Dollar where once Mary, Queen of Scots, had been a prisoner. The girl was telling Sara about a love affair that hadn't turned out well. I overheard her say, "Oh, he was a MacGregor, but I won't have to tell you any more. Sure, you have read *Rob Roy* and know what they are. There never was a MacGregor was not a rogue." A rogue, by the bye, has a severity of meaning in Scotland. It means an out-and-out rascal and good-for-nothing. I learned afterward that she had got together her trousseau and everything was ready for the marriage when they found out things about him that prevented the marriage.

We listened to the bagpipes as a sickle moon rode over the Ochills. We bought the collops in the village, we walked home again, and sat up until midnight talking.

The next day we called on Mr. Malcolm, of the Dollar

Institution. It was he who told me he had tried thirteen
signs on me and I responded to none of them. He was a
"jiner." It was there when we visited the power plant of
the Dollar Institution that the engineer asked me, "Is it
from the University of Pennsylvania where Hillprecht has
made the Babylonian collections you come?" Scotland was
Scotland running true to form as the land of learning.
That Sabbath afternoon at the Dollar Institution I lost
the little regard Mrs. Malcolm had for me when I asked
for water for my whisky. By the bye, the dear little boys of
the Dollar Institution had to serve whisky to the guests of
their headmaster on the Sabbath afternoon, whisky that
should have been taken straight. There is very little
whisky I can take straight, and no Scotch.

That morning as we walked with Mr. Malcolm we
passed the Episcopal minister leading a chow dog. He was
a red chow. He opened his mouth and I saw it was all
black inside. That was the first chow dog of my acquaintance. As I was admiring the dog, Mr. Malcolm, a staunch
Presbyterian, said, "The deeseenting minister."

It was here we learned that Robert Louis Stevenson had
come to Dollar to do a topographical chart as an engineering student in the University of Edinburgh. A day or two
before the chart was due, Stevenson copied what another
boy had surveyed. We were told it was none too well done
and Stevenson's copy was not accepted. Stevenson had
stayed at a little place called "The Yetts of Muckart"—that
is, the Gates of Muckart. It was the toll gate.

From Dollar we went to Edinburgh, loveliest of cities,
with Holyrood to the one side and the Crag to the other,
and the trumpet at evening sounding from the army bar-
racks. Here we stayed at a temperance hotel, cheap, clean,
and most disheartening. I remember we went out very
late of a Saturday night and bought Devonshire cream and

strawberries, though it was now September, and had an orgy in our rooms. We had had scant pickings at the supper table that night.

We went south from Edinburgh straight through to London with no stop, seeing only Durham Cathedral and a picturesque canal boat pulled by a lone horse on the way south. I should have liked to stop at York and to have visited the tombstone of James Thomas, my grandfather Morgan Jones Thomas' brother, who died from cholera. He had been taken into his house by a doctor named Belcomb. It was thus that Belcomb came into the Thomas family as a name, Uncle Jim being James Belcomb Thomas, and his son again James Belcomb Thomas.

From London we went down to Alton and Selborne, Gilbert White's country. I have made record of this in "A Selborne Pilgrimage" reprinted in *Tuesdays at Ten*. It appeared first in the *Atlantic Monthly* in 1904. We saw Chawton and other places associated with Jane Austen and arrived in Winchester the day that Hyde Abbey was taken over by the government. It was then camped in by gypsies and other people of the roads. They were picking hops down in the Hampshire country, these gypsies and the scum from London. The gypsies we were told were a much better lot than the cockneys. We moved on to Oxford and from Oxford down to Liverpool. When we got into the Liverpool train at the junction near Oxford we found an English couple occupying the whole of the compartment in which we had seats bought and paid for. The guard had evidently been tipped to let them occupy the whole compartment. He merely ushered us to the door of the compartment and fled. Both the seat facing forward and the seat facing backward were filled. Next to the window facing the engine sat very much of a gentleman who afterward turned out to be a lord who had been an officer of parts in the South African campaign. He had many pictures of little Boer girls which he was trying to show to the lady sitting opposite to him, who was his wife. All she would talk about, however, was whether she ought to have his monogram combined with hers on her cigarette paper or not. This, of course, we learned afterward. First, there had to be our making our way into our seats.

I said to the man, "I beg your pardon, but I hold two seats for this compartment." He gave me a stony stare. I seized a bit of baggage and put it under the seat facing the engine, not, of course, the preferable seat according to English choice. The preferred seat is with your back to the engine because that entails less smoke blowing into you than would blow into you if you sat in the seat facing the engine. There was nothing for the man to do but to put some of his impedimenta under the seat. We had very little luggage. He looked very ashamed of himself for his attempt to hog the compartment. I suppose he had been told to.

About six months after this, and when we were home, I read that she had divorced him. Apparently he hadn't seen his wife for a long, long time. It must have been a very, very difficult situation to face. She was evidently giving him the cold shoulder and he was trying to be pleasant to carry it off. Of course I didn't know of any incipient trouble between them or I might have felt differently about our butting in, but I did butt in and successfully and I got the seats I paid for.

There was not much that was interesting on the way back. There was the shifting of the cargo and the wonderment as to what might happen should we run into such storms as we had crossing from Philadelphia to Liverpool in July. It was good again to see the electric lights of Atlantic City, and Wildwood, and Cape May.

There was an interesting moment when we arrived in Philadelphia. It was a hot afternoon late in September. Father had driven in for us with the team. The customs officers were divided among the people, but those of us at the end of the alphabet were left out. I went over to where a very *dégagé* gentleman sitting in what was strangely like a cashier's stand at a country fair looked to the ceiling of the wharf house. I said, "I have the misfortune to have a name beginning with W. My folks have driven in for me from Germantown."

At the word Germantown his whole attitude changed. He looked down at me fiercely and said, "Did you say Germantown?"

I said, "Yes, we come from Germantown."

"So do I," he said, and then smiling benignly and seizing a piece of chalk, he slid down from his eminence and walked over and said, "These your trunks?"

I said, "Yes."

"Shut them up."

I shut them up. He marked them "passed" with the chalk. I then thought of all that I might have brought in that I had not brought in. For once coming from Germantown was an asset.

CHAPTER 13

TEACHER TALKS SHOP

IT WOULD be easy to recast into the running narrative in which most of this book is written a talk I gave in the spring of 1938. It may break the monotony of all, however, if I leave it in the spoken discourse in which I delivered it. Here is what I said:

Fellow teachers: I hope I have the right to call myself teacher. I hope I am right in calling you teachers. Yesterday you had to be teachers, for yesterday you of the schools had to teach to prepare your students to pass examinations we of the colleges set. Now, of course, we are completely in your hands. We take the students you certify to us and they are as good in every respect save manners as those students of yesterday who had to pass examinations. It is more certain you are teachers than that I am. Nearly forty years ago a little woman teaching in a school not thirty miles from Philadelphia said to me, of the colleges as opposed to herself of the schools: "You lecture. We teach." The iron entered my soul with that remark. From that time on I was conscious that I had to burn it in on my classes. Instead of merely harmlessly lecturing at them I made what I had to say clear enough, full enough of concrete illustrations, human enough, happy enough, said over and over enough times to be remembered.

This old teacher talks shop from his years of experience. He is not too sure of the effects of his teaching. Certainly those he has taught have not always remembered his teaching. He who has never taught, save in an outline or type course, any literature earlier than that of the nineteenth century, and whose specialty is contemporary English literature, is told by a graduate of thirty years' standing how fondly that graduate remembers a course he had with teacher in Shakespeare, a course teacher never taught.

As common is this experience. A boy comes into class a week late on the eve of the First World War. He says: "I was waved in here by the American flag. I served down on the border of Mexico and so won rating that admitted me to college. I tried four times to pass the entrance examinations after studying on my own. I failed four times. When I finally got in, I wanted to get courses that wouldn't get me up too early in the morning. I have never liked to get up. I looked at the roster. I found there an unforbidding name, Owen, but he gave English Forty at nine o'clock. I saw there a name I couldn't even pronounce, W-e-y-g-a-n-d-t. That name was at ten o'clock. That was all there was in its favor. A boy came by. I said to him: 'What kind of a guy is this named W-e-y-g-a-n-d-t?' The fellow I questioned sort of heaved a sigh and said, 'Well, he's not so bad as some of the others.' So here I am."

It is the little incident in the classroom or the asides that most students remember. Years back we had two boys playing the two ends on our football team. One of them was named Crooks and the other Braddock. Both were up-state boys, Williamsport way. In these old days of smaller classes teacher called the roll. I called, "Braddock." I heard Mr. Crooks feigning Mr. Braddock's voice. I didn't even look up. I knew Crooks was answering for him. About the time I finished calling the roll Braddock appeared at the door. He didn't come up to his regular seat because he didn't wish to interrupt teacher talking. At the end of the hour he began to make his way up to tell me he was present. Crooks made demonstrations to him to shoo him away. Braddock didn't notice the demonstrations. He came up and said, "I came in late." I said, "That's all right, Mr. Braddock, you were vicariously present when your name was called." Crooks, hovering around, was in some confusion. He was a fair boy with blushing cheeks and the blushes had extended from the center of his cheeks up to his eyes and forehead. I didn't catch his eye.

I meet Mr. Crooks every now and then. The first time I remember meeting him after college was in the restaurant in the Nineteenth Street Market. He was sitting opposite me alongside of the largest man I had ever seen. He finished before I did and moved out. Suddenly I felt a hand on my shoulder and looking around there was Mr. Crooks presenting this huge man. He said, "Dr. Weygandt, I have here Tiny Roebuck. I was telling him about how you caught me answering for Braddock years ago. He said he'd like to meet the man who had so good an ear he could distinguish one boy's voice from another, so here he is." A huge paw was extended which seemed to wrap round my hand several times. My hand was paralyzed by that grip. I didn't believe that this could be so great a man as Tiny Roebuck, the wrestler, but so it was. I thought at first that it was just Mr. Crooks playboying, but it was the real Tiny Roebuck, the only wrestler I ever had the honor of meeting. I love to listen to them on the radio, Mr. Londos, Mr. Detton, Mr. Orville Brown, Chief Little Wolf, Mr. Everette Marshall, and all those heroes of yesteryear, Jim Browning, Dick Shikat, Yvon Robert, the O'Mahoney, Crusher Casey, Joe Stecher, and their ilk.

There are many pleasant things to remember. I am driving from my summer home in North Sandwich, New Hampshire, down to Ossipee Court House with my neighbor, Charles Fellows. A car runs by our faithful Ford and cuts across in front of us. I almost collide with it when I jam on the brakes. I say, "It has happened at last, it's a hold-up." I am preparing to get out my wallet and hand it over when I see the grinning face of a boy from Wilmington in Delaware. He says, "Oh, Dr. Weygandt, pardon me for stopping you, but I did want you to meet my parents. We are on our way up to Moosehead Lake." I was hauled over and presented to Mamma and Papa.

On Chestnut Street a man no more than ten years my junior is coming upstreet as I am going down. He breaks through the moving throng of people and says, "Will you give me that line of Yeats that tells about the boy going back home and finding the girl who was just a child become woman and altogether irresistible?" I say, "You mean, 'She put on womanhood, and he lost peace.'"

Black alder, that deciduous holly they sell on the streets before Christmas, its leaves gone and the red berries standing out against the black twigs, is of deep appeal to me. A man of forty will put his hand on my shoulder as I am looking over bunches of it and say, "Robert Frost's favorite black alder."

Another boy, a potentate of Hollywood, will get into the car and say, "Do you remember that day you came into Two-o-five with a copy of *The English Review* in your hands and said, 'I have here a long poem by John Masefield. Do you remember his *Salt Water Ballads?*' Well, he's done it again and in a larger way."

You get out of the train to buy some greengage plums in Oregon. A boy comes up and says, "Dr. Weygandt, isn't it? Are you still teaching Ninety-one and giving Bernard Shaw what is coming to him? Do you still call him 'the apostle of the half educated'?" I did then in 1923 and I do still.

My deep interest in schoolteaching and my concern with it is not only because of my own years at it but because so many of my forbears were in it and so many of my family associated with it. I am fairly environed and beset with schoolteachers. My wife was a schoolteacher, my mother was a schoolteacher, my mother's father was a schoolteacher. In the house of my great-great-great-great-grandfather was held one of the early meetings for the foundation of a school in Germantown. It is old Johannes Bechtel of whom I am speaking. Coming down to more recent times, my son is a schoolteacher and my daughter, too.

It is some fifteen thousand have suffered me as a teacher at Pennsylvania. It seems to me that suffering cannot be as great on their part distributed among that number as is the suffering I have endured from the fifteen thousand. However, we have borne one another bravely, if not cheerfully. What is the first requisite of a teacher? Before knowledge of his subject, before clarity of exposition, before the repetition of whatever he has to teach six times and the hope that someone in the class will remember after the six times, is the necessity to suffer a fool gladly. One must be indifferent to the student pulling the watch on you. That hardens my heart a little. When I see a boy at that I catch his eye and say as an aside, "I will keep all of you a minute longer than the regular time for that." I have always thought there ought to be a clock in every lecture room above teacher's head. It would help the manners of the taught. And, by the bye, when you have them read anything to their classmates always teach them to turn each page over face downward as they read so the rest of the class and yourself may observe the diminishing pile of manuscript. I have no manuscript tonight so you can't have that joy and there are none of you know just how long the man will talk. I never let any student read a paper that lasts for more than twenty minutes, but I have been

HENRY REED

HENRY D. THOREAU

COLLEGE HALL, UNIVERSITY OF PENNSYLVANIA
FROM A PLATE OF THE 1890's

told that you must have tonight a double dose of twenty, forty. Perhaps I will be a little easy on you and stop at thirty, and perhaps I won't.

There is running through my memory a sort of refrain sprung, of course, of Kipling's. "I learned about women from her." I learned about teaching from him, or, I beg your pardon, from her. I am one of the first of the kindergarten taught. I sat under Maria Gay. I remember very little of that because I was only four. I remember very well six and sitting under Elizabeth Head. Mrs. Head had a dame school in Germantown in which there were both small boys and small girls. The boys moved on at ten. I was in her school perhaps for three years or four. One of my colleagues was delivered of the memorable dictum "It is better to be clear than to be right." Just as necessary is the doctrine, repeated six times, be concrete, be concrete, be concrete, be concrete, be concrete, be concrete. Give a concrete illustration of every point you are trying to make.

I remember teaching I sat under at Pennsylvania. There I met the greatest teacher I ever sat under in my young years, Robert Ellis Thompson. I'll remember that cold drafty room on the fourth floor of College Hall for as long as I am. When we came into the room for what was supposed to be a course in the Norman occupation of England, Dominie Thompson, good Irishman from Lurgan, would greet us with the calling of the roll. He had it by heart. He would recite from Ashhurst to Yarnall with scarcely looking at the roll unless the boy happened not to be there and he had to mark him absent.

One day one of the boys, when he was discussing the spelling of names, asked him why he spelled his name Thompson, instead of Thomson, as did the writer of *The Seasons*. "Huh, I spell it Thompson," replied Dominie Thompson, "with a P for Presbyterian, P for Presbyterian!" He was a Presbyterian minister and a teacher of teachers. It was from Thompson and from an essay by Matthew Arnold in which he speaks of the necessity of repetition that I have my doctrine of saying everything six times and hoping someone will remember. I used to gather up the notebooks from my lectures, but I found from what was put down in them that I was disseminating so much misinformation that I quit. I liked to think, of course, that I said the thing truly enough but that the taught were fallible and got it crooked.

After all, no matter what schemes or methods or theories of teaching are followed in this school or that, in the last analysis it is up to the teacher. When our English Department does things which I think are not for the betterment of our teaching, I always console myself with the reflection: "Even the English Department cannot stop the English Department." I mean, of course, that granted we have the men that we have, vagaries imposed upon us really do not much hinder. It is a difficult matter to strait-jacket a good teacher into ineffectiveness by even the most advanced methods.

I am delighted that today we are passing out of that theory of self-expression which has been for a half generation at any rate the bane of American youth. What we want is not self-expression. What we want is so to teach that the taught will be so full of the subject, so possessed by that which they are taught that they will utterly forget self. It is with writing as it is with teaching. The subject a man writes about must possess the man. If it's only the man possessing the subject he will be a posturing, attitudinizing, play-acting bore. I have heaped up the adjectives to make the thing as repulsive as it is. Composition writing is the finding of material. If the boy can be completely possessed by the subject he is writing about, he will, if he has been rightly taught, forget himself and let himself be but the mouthpiece through which the subject speaks.

The teacher is the interpreter, the middleman. I am proud to belong to an institution in which Henry Reed from 1835 to 1854 middlemanned Wordsworth and Thackeray to America. I am proud to have had my little part in middlemanning Yeats and Synge, Conrad and Masefield to America, and Robert Frost, too, to his own country. One remembers one's intentions and wishes that one's results were within hailing distance of those intentions. One remembers one's breaks. One remembers one's being put in one's place by resolute ladies of some summers. One day a bat came into a room in which I was teaching in the College Courses for Teachers, as we called them then. It fluttered around and around, much to the distress of the many ladies and much to the delight of the few men in the room. I opened a window and thought maybe it would escape, feeling the current of air. It did not. A managing woman, all in black, rose majestically from her place far in the rear of the room and paraded up the aisle to the right and opened a window opposite the window I had opened. The bat then felt the current of air and sailed out the window I had opened. The lady did not even gaze upon me in triumph. She was very tolerant of the crass stupidity of man, as, fortunately, most ladies are.

One learns from noticing how older teachers meet embarrassing situations. I had my class in freshman composition writing one day in Room 214 College Hall, University of Pennsylvania. Across the hall from 214 was 206 where Professor Blank taught Mathematics. Nineteen-one Mechanical and Electrical Engineers were having calculus with Professor Blank. There were two doors to the room.

The boys formed an unbroken circle and marched lockstep out one door and in the other. The door of my room was open to the hall and I could see right out and across into the other room. Professor Blank had been in consultation with a student at his desk. He noticed the circle and walked out into the hall alongside of its revolving line of boys. He began keeping time with them, stamping his feet and clapping his hands. He said, "Gentlemen, you march lockstep fery vell, but not quite goot enough for chail yet." The circle was broken, the boys broke into applause, and took their seats quietly in the room.

One has certain embarrassing moments in the classroom. On the morning after the night on which we all went wild on the false alarm of the ending of the first World War, a pretty girl went to sleep in my classroom. A number of the boys had, and, by the bye, Number one, Number two, and Number three of the boys who went to sleep in my classroom died shortly after their nappings. So I always hold them up as examples of what might happen to others who fall asleep in my classroom. I told the girl her days were numbered. I had had this girl's father in class before her and she had handed me a composition that her dad had handed in twenty years before. He was a doctor down Jersey. I recognized the composition and told her to tell Dad that teacher had risen to the bait. This was a class that some of my younger colleagues had wished on me that I might learn how much harder was their job now that they were teaching composition than had been mine in the good old days when I had been teaching composition. They had gathered together what they regarded as an aggregation of undesirables, but it turned out, as it so often does, that most of the ugly duckling were swans.

It has, of course, been the code from the beginning of time that teacher was an abstracted unpractical kind of person who really didn't see what was going on in the class-room at all. As a matter of fact, as you all know, the good teacher intentionally fails to see a good deal that goes on in the classroom. One never knows what's going on be-hind the talking that disturbs us sometimes. Once in a large class of about two hundred and fifty boys I was dis-turbed by talking. I stopped talking to wait for two boys in the back of the room to come to quiet. At the end of the hour one of them came up to apologize. He said, "What was happening was this. You noticed maybe I came in a little late. I had been hunting the fellow I sat next to. He comes from my home town. I had been hunting him because I had had a letter from home saying the girl to whom he was engaged had married another man. I was just breaking word to him as diplomatically as I could and what interrupted you was his blurting out an 'Oh, hell.' "

I said, "Tell the boy he's lucky. No boy in college is old enough to know whether he can be happily annexed by a girl. The girl who jilts a boy in college does him a serv-ice." That is the rough consolation I always offer when I am father confessor to boys in that particular kind of trouble. It hurts, but the hearts of young folks heal rapidly.

Yes, we who are teachers have our troubles the same as another. We haven't allowed those troubles, however, to prevent us doing our jobs and in many instances doing more than our jobs. We can do other things than teach. I know an incomparable teacher who delights alumni re-unions of his classes by standing on his head. He has so delighted classes for thirty years. Other teachers can write. Robert Frost, for instance, was a teacher who taught Eng-lish so well at the Derry Academy in southern New Hamp-shire that he was asked to teach psychology in the State Teachers College at Plymouth, New Hampshire. There he found teachers from country districts who thought there would be a study of hypnotism in courses in psychology. One girl had heard that if you would hypnotize a class and then tell it something while it was under hypnosis it would remember it forever. Perhaps that's the way out for those of us who teach. Perhaps some process like that of hypnosis will come our way and what we teach will be remembered willy-nilly.

We are called upon to do so much more than our predecessors a generation or two ago were called upon to do. Then we had in America family tradition and most of our students were children from families of a certain amount of cultivation. Now children of all sorts find their way to school and college. We are asked to supply that family tradition of yesterday or day before yesterday, a tradition that is wanting today. Teaching cannot do that. It cannot take the place of family tradition. One of the reasons that we are not advancing in cultivation in America is because of this decay of family tradition. It is unreasonable to expect us to supply that which the parents should give their children. The old headmaster under whom I studied at the Germantown Academy, William Kershaw, always used to say that he ran as good a school as the parents of his students would allow him to run.

You in the schools are fortunate in that research work and publication are not demanded of you as they are of us in the colleges. You are forced into administrative work, but you are not forced to give up all your spare time to the preparation of articles that show your competence in some little field of research. There is no question that to be a great teacher you must have time to live. Do not most of us question with Matthew Arnold:

> What shelter to grow ripe is ours?
> What leisure to grow wise?

We should have time for reading, for travel, time to loaf
and invite our souls. Life should not be all study, all work,
or all playing at play. First of all is the necessity of meeting
all sorts and conditions of people, not just people of our
own kind, but people of less ordered and regimented lives.
One must have human sympathy, sympathy with people
who look at things from other viewpoints than our own.
There is a freshness about such people that is as stimulat-
ing as April air or as is, on an August noon, the water of
a pond fed by springs.

There is not yet in the world a sufficient appreciation
of the real teacher. There is no need of any man to be
more than a teacher, one who has the privilege of opening up the wonders of a subject to an awaking mind. After
all, men and women taken as a whole are never better
than in their school and college years. Some go on growing all life through, but too many are got the better of
by the world. John Masefield has a line devastatingly true
about "The self that withers like a flower." I meet many
old students, some of whom have got the better of both
themselves and the world, others of whom have sold their
souls to the world for a mess of pottage.

They do kindly things to you, old students. I go up to
Princeton to talk at the Nassau Club and a civil engineer
I have not met for thirty years insists on driving me all
the way home. He talks all the way. That man does not
give himself away by that talk. Or perhaps I should say he
gives himself away only to his credit. I go out the Juniata
to talk at Huntingdon and I am carried out to a country
club. Even with the free tongue that dining and wining
bring about, that old student remains the gentleman I
knew in the classroom and in conferences in my office. Before all my spare time was taken up with writing, I played
father confessor to many youths. I was told by one student

that I was in the wrong profession. I should have been a Catholic priest because I would be easy to tell sins to.

What are the sins to which the world tempts so many able men? Power over their fellow men, through money, through business positions, through political maneuvers. Through ambition for such power they "go along," they take orders because only by doing so, they say, they can get things done. They forget that great line that Pope handed on to Burns: "An honest man's the noblest work of God." The last time I met Owen Roberts, Mr. Justice Roberts of the Supreme Court of the United States, he came over to me and said, "I still think, Corney, the greatest line of English poetry is 'An honest man's the noblest work of God.'"

The successful lawyer who has sacrificed his standards for that success looks at his old teacher furtively when, in a conference, he is caught in a lie. May we all so live that our pupils cannot but respect us, cannot but look back to the days with us in the classroom as good and happy days. If we have given of ourselves to them as the best teachers do, we members of the most unselfish profession in the world, the men and women who were our students cannot but remember us with a glow in the heart. They will do that if we have gone to our classrooms with enthusiasm and happiness, if we have shown that there is such a thing as delight in learning, if we have been firmly convinced that our first duty, after suffering fools gladly, is to bring happiness into the classroom as well as learning. I would have written on the walls of every room in our broad land in which there is teaching, from little red schoolhouse, if such there be today a going concern, to the largest lecture room in every university in the land, the legend: "The days that make us happy make us wise."

CHAPTER 14

OF TALK AND TALKING

ALL my people could talk vigorously in conversation but none of them I knew were public speakers. Old Johannes Bechtel, I suppose, had some powers of eloquence, or he could not have occupied the pulpit for as long as he did back in the second quarter of the eighteenth century. My gift of the gab came from both Weygandts and Thomas', but my roar was developed by the necessities of my teaching job. When I was a boy at college we had to take "elocution," to talk in the dim chapel of so poor acoustics our voices would come echoing back to us as we orated the round periods of Henry Clay and Daniel Webster. Professor McElroy did one of his students a great service, as I have already recorded, when he said to us in class: "Young gentlemen! Be aware of your diaphragms."

I thought of that when I began teaching in 1897. Until I had recaptured the art of speaking from my chest I grew tired and hoarse after several hours' teaching. I began with seventeen hours a week, with Friday's five hours constituting my hardest day. It did not take me long, fortunately, to get the knack of it again, but every September on returning to talking in public after a summer with little of public speaking in it, it takes me about a week to bring my voice under control again.

I was slow in becoming an effective public speaker. I was always fluent enough, but it took me a long while to learn how to remember what I wanted to say without notes before me. I had never really had proper instruction in the matter. Robert Ellis Thompson, by example, and not by precept, taught me something of what I should do. I was easy before my college classes from about my seventh month of teaching, but it was twenty years after 1897 before I was utterly composed before a great audience. My Commencement Day address in 1922, "The Heritage of Pennsylvania," marked the beginning of competency on such occasions. This address was made in Weightman Hall, and I was told my voice, unassisted by amplification, reached all the way to the rear of that building and was heard by all the three thousand people sitting in the great hall. When I gave the commencement address again, in 1934, on "Seven Byways to Happiness," amplifiers were used, and my voice reached all the ten thousand present.

It may be that raucousness is what makes my voice carry so well. A colleague of mine was driven from his den by the "boom" of it. His family insisted on hearing what I was saying over the radio, and he fled upstairs and shut all the doors between him and the radio. My "heresies," he said, searched him out even in his third-story retreat. When I return to Sandwich in late June after a winter in which I have talked over the radio some of the neighbors are sure to say: "Well, we heard your old familiar voice on the air last winter."

It is a powerful voice, and carries well, even if it is "raucous" or "booming." I should prefer other adjectives, but even if these prevail I accept them. I repeat what I have said before, that time and again, when I have talked, someone comes up to me and says with great enthusiasm: "I could hear you." That may not be a great compliment, but it brings home the fact, unfortunate but true, that, without amplification, most speakers cannot be heard. You can hear every word I say, even if I talk too fast, sometimes up to two hundred words a minute. I am the despair of stenographers when I go full tilt.

I have done a good deal of speaking in my time, at alumni meetings; women's clubs; college and school commencements; at functions of the Union League and Sons of the Revolution in Philadelphia; at dinners of this denomination or that, Presbyterian, Lutheran, Schwenkfelder; at librarians' conventions; and at Old Home Day meetings. I have spoken out-of-doors on some of these occasions, but I have always been heard. I know, of course, how to "throw my voice," and I have a voice to throw.

Of my talks to alumni they like best that which recounts what I have seen happen in College Hall, amusing incidents in the classroom, moments of vision that came to teacher there, praise of Pennsylvania men of old years that I have come to know through tradition, or through sitting under in my young years. "Poets Off Parade" is as popular a talk as I have made before the women's clubs, gossip of the poets I have met since Samuel Wentworth Longfellow used to walk down to the Germantown Academy to walk up Greene Street with the boys. There is talk of Whitman in this "lecture," of Yeats and Russell and James Stephens, of Noyes and Masefield and Laurence Binyon, of Vachel Lindsay and Frost, of Dunsany and Higgins and Ralph Hodgson.

I have talked at meetings of various Irish groups both in Philadelphia and New York, meeting Douglas Hyde and Joseph Campbell, and having a courteous hearing even when my admiration of Synge and Yeats ran counter to the feeling of the men before whom I spoke. I have had to do a good deal of speaking for which I have not been paid before local historical groups and associations of teachers and neighbors' clubs. I prefer twenty-minute talks to talks any longer, but I can "go strong" for an hour.

Many of the chapters of my books have been originally talks, and I have often talked chapters of the books after they have been put into print. *The Red Hills* has brought me talks in Lancaster, Harrisburg, Lebanon, Reading, York, Allentown, Bethlehem, Lansdale, and Norristown. One of the most successful talks on things Pennsylvania Dutch I call "On the Trail of the Tulip." It is a following through all household art of the use of the tulip as a decorative motive, a talk parallel to the later one on the rose delivered at Manheim. I have talked on Jacob Eichholtz, the painter, on the unveiling of a tablet at the house in which he lived at Lancaster. I have been asked to talk at family reunions at various places in the Dutch country, but such meetings have always occurred during the summer months when I have been in New Hampshire.

In New Hampshire I have always talked when asked to in Sandwich, but I have charged for talks ouside of Sandwich, at Wolfeboro, say, and at Exeter. Demands for talks there, outside of my home town, have come from folks who have read my New Hampshire books. The books, or old students, have taken me to Westfield and New Brunswick, Trenton and Atlantic City in New Jersey, and down the eastern shore of Maryland to Salisbury. Some of these trips have brought to my attention things to write about, but talking is such hard work I have never gone out of my way to do it. I am not a joiner of any sort and what talks have come my way have come from people who really wanted me.

One of the most amusing chores that ever came my way was as a result of a plea years back to go to a little college in Pennsylvania and "make drama intellectually respectable." For once I must have done my chore fairly well, for a very distinguished scholar beat the table in high approval at what I said and came to me after the banquet

TWO NEW HAMPSHIRE NEIGHBORS
LOUIS ELLIOT AND HIS BEAR

Photograph by William K. Beard, Jr.

DURGIN BRIDGE, NORTH SANDWICH, N. H.

was over to say: "At last I have heard myself talk." That was, perhaps, the highest compliment I ever received. My way of talking has been adopted, I have already said, by a number of my old students teaching hither and yon. Those that follow my methods most closely seldom have me talk in their bailiwicks, but I find out about their adoption of my ways by students who come to Pennsylvania as transfers from these institutions. A boy will wait about after one of my hours, come up to me and say: "You taught So-and-So, did you not?" and chuckle as he goes away saying: "I thought so."

I have come gradually to a very definite way of preparing my talks. As I have never seen this method recorded in print, I put it down for what it is worth. I write out the whole speech word for word. I rewrite the whole of it again in longhand. Then I have it copied in typescript. Then I make an outline in two columns on ordinary typewriter paper and have that pasted on a sheet of thin cardboard. This I fold down the middle so it will slip into the pocket of my coat. I try to get the outline clearly in mind. That is not generally very difficult, for the outline has generally a logical development. I take the completely written-out speech with me in case I need it in an emergency. I never refer to it, and to the outline very seldom, only to be sure I do not leave out one of the seven parts into which my Gaul is divided. I always write out a longer speech than I need, so that there will be plenty to fill out the time even if I neglect a minor point here or there.

I have found that an intimate talk can be put over even to a great assembly of people, as my "Seven Byways to Happiness" went over to the ten thousand at the Pennsylvania commencement in Convention Hall in 1934. Though I am the survivor of literally hundreds of public talks I am never sure a certain talk is going to go over. It does three times out of four, but I have had the experience of an old talk, tried and true, that has scored with one audience, failing to score with another audience. Sometimes I can tell why the talk fails to score, but more often I cannot.

CHAPTER 15

CELEBRITIES

YEATS came to America in 1903, the year after we had met him in Ireland. We had Dr. Horace Howard Furness to introduce him and filled Houston Hall for the talk and reading. Yeats was very poet in appearance, and that appearance helped considerably to make the occasion memorable. He talked and read not more than pretty well. After his three months' tour across the country he did very much better. It had taken him only that short three months of his absence in the West to master the art of talking about Ireland and of reading his verse. He came back to us two or three times after this, but he never outdid the effect he made on that first appearance before he was master of the art. John Quinn invited me over to New York to a dinner he gave for the poet just before he sailed for home in 1904. That was my first meeting with a representative group of Irish-American notables. They could nearly all talk well.

Lady Gregory came along with the company from the Abbey Theatre in 1911-12. She was a dignified figure. She talked very well in the Houston Club on the riots over the *Playboy* and of the dramatic movement in Ireland generally. Her best play, *Grania*, is now forgotten and time has had its way with her farces. She was adept at damnings. She spoke of Seumas MacManus as "Shame Us MacManus." I had heard him talk. He was very pedagogue, petulant and a dull speaker.

I wrote to Robert Frost about his verse in 1915. We had summered first in New Hampshire, in Birch Interval, in

1912, and we went back there again in 1915. We drove up to Franconia with Mr. and Mrs. Charles Matlack to call on the Frosts in the late summer of 1915. We brought him down to Philadelphia the following winter to talk at Pennsylvania and before the Science and Art Clubs of Germantown at our house. I have known him well ever since, though we meet perhaps only every third year. He dropped in upon us in May of 1938 for a part of a day between readings at Washington and Meadville. He and Mrs. Frost were with us in Sandwich for three days in 1934. Their first visit to us in New Hampshire had been in 1916 while we still summered in Win Kimball's cottage in Birch Interval. What I think of the poet I have said in *The White Hills*. I have had the best of talk from the man. I know well nobody more interesting. I am proud to write myself down "Servant to Pennsylvania and friend of Robert Frost."

Masefield came to lecture to us in the great hall of the gymnasium in 1916. I had written him about *The Street of Today*. There I found an anachronism, mention of buff Orpington fowls as picking about in a hen run years before the Orpingtons were selected from cross-bred buff Cochins, Cochins without feathers on their legs. I had a short note from him saying he had my note re Orpingtons and would investigate. When I met him at the Franklin Inn Club I introduced myself as the man from New Hampshire who had written to him about Orpingtons. "Ah!" he said. "You were quite right about that, but there never came another edition for me to change it in. Where will I get a setting of eggs of the brown African goose?"

I put my hand in my pocket and picked out a circular from Charles McClave, I think it was, of Illyria, Ohio, advertising brown African geese. As I was in our lane on my way to take train for town I had met the postman, who gave me what of our mail was addressed to me. Among it was McClave's circular. Masefield never batted an eyelash over his question so completely answered, nor did I.

Masefield heard that these geese matured more quickly than any others and would therefore prove a help in provisioning England, then much harried by the U-boat raids. A setting finally went to him, carried over, if I remember rightly, by Roy Pardee, of Islip, Long Island, when he went over with some of our troops. I never heard if they arrived safely, and hatched, and began a new strain of brown African geese in old England.

I am no collector of autographs, but I had brought along my copy of *Salt Water Ballads,* his first book and a rare collector's item, for him to sign. He said: "Where shall I sign it?"

I said, "Under 'Sea Fever.' "

He replied: "Thank you! It's the best thing in the book."

When he read in the gymnasium I introduced him. It was supposed to be a reading, but he ran in a running narrative of this and that between the sets of verse, telling many incidents of a monkey he had sailed with on some ship. He had said to me before he began to read: "Will you watch how they stand it? If they can stand another poem, say 'Poem,' won't you, and if they cannot, say 'Jocko.' " He shot to me after each poem a ventriloquist's "Poem or Jocko?" I said every time: "Poem," and the hour went over as a great success. He was as modest a distinguished man as I had ever met.

I had first seen him at the Contemporary Club, where, a year before he read, he had been violently attacked as a vulgarian by the very people who now crowded around him as a great celebrity. That attack had so outraged Dave Wallerstein that he had excitedly hunted around, but

vainly, for a copy of Masefield's poems so he could con-
fute the detractors by reading aloud from the poet. Masefield read before Pennsylvania another time, but I cannot
remember whether that was before or after the Jocko
reading. The reading this other time had been scheduled
for the Houston Club but that little auditorium was so
crowded and so great a crowd was milling all about it that
the reading was transferred to the Asbury Methodist Episcopal Church, on Chestnut Street above Thirty-third, and
that, too, was filled to overflowing.

I had heard Vachel Lindsay read a couple of times before he came to Houston Hall and had us growl with him
in his "rendition" of his "Daniel in the Lion's Den"
verses. One of these earlier readings was at Wharton Stork's
over on the Old York Road. It was a Sunday afternoon, if
I remember rightly, and Vachel was resplendent in a yellow shirt with a pink collar and bright green necktie. I
liked the whole-souled and hearty man he was more than I
liked his poetry. The "Congo" with its "fat black bucks"
I liked, and the Rachel Jane passages of "The Santa Fe
Trail," but his Altgeld verses and those describing the
young folks going down to the railroad station in prairie
Illinois of a Sunday afternoon I liked better. I shall never
forget how shocked one of my colleagues was at the steam
siren verses with their "Calliope, shouting hope." When
Lindsay began that my old friend could stand it no more
but broke from the hall in disgust and fled home.

James Stephens came to us to read from his writing in
1925. I had got my signals crossed and arranged for his
reading on the afternoon of the day on the morning of
which my better half's niece was to be married. I had to
cut a class, which I hate to do, to meet the Stephens' at
North Philadelphia. There emerged from the sleeper a
redcap carrying about nine items of luggage, a little lady

carrying two small bags, and last a leprechaun of a man drifting wistfully along without impedimenta. I broke it to them immediately about the wedding, asking them whether they would go home to our house for a sleep after the trying night in the sleeper or whether they would go to the wedding. Mrs. Stephens replied promptly: "We shall go to the wedding. I have never been to an American wedding."

We went to the wedding and then to his reading. Though he was struck with a panic before it, he got through with it very well and he was wildly applauded by the audience. As I have written of all this visit of Stephens in detail in "Poets Off Parade," I write no more of it here. I have written of him critically in "The Riddling of James Stephens" in *Tuesdays at Ten*, in *A Century of the English Novel*, and in *The Time of Yeats*, so I shall have little to say of his art here. The pity of it is that he is of those many writers that have only their ten years. What he promised in verse appears in *Insurrections* (1909). His last book of parts is *Irish Fairy Tales* (1920). *The Charwoman's Daughter* (1912), *The Crock of Gold* (1913), and *The Demi-Gods* (1914) are the best of him. It was the end of him when he left Ireland, as it was the end of O'Casey.

I heard George W. Russell talk at the Contemporary Club when he came to Philadelphia. His talks represented Ireland so other than the Ireland I knew I had not the heart to go up and speak to him at the end of his talk. The appeal of his personality was still as great as when we met him in Dublin in 1902, but his talk was completely that of the politician. He held his appeal, however, for most people to the end. Dunsany said to me of him in 1928, "Nothing he can say can prevent him being the best man and the first power for good in Ireland." I hope he was that, for he missed being a poet of moment. I was utterly taken with his verses in my younger years, but I found him out in my middle years, and he shrinks to a very short stature as I look out on poetry from the vantage point of old age.

Francis Brett Young came to Pennsylvania to talk. He is to me the best of the novelists of the generation later than Moore and Conrad. He stands the test of the years better than Galsworthy, who except for *A Man of Property* seems today but a topical writer. Brett Young writes well. The pity is he has had to write for his living, he has had to write too much. *The Redlakes,* however, and *The House under the Water* are close to great novels. Only time will tell whether they are great novels or not. He is pre-eminently the gentleman, that before all else save the man of words. He does not write of his characters as medical cases as Maugham does always, and as A. J. Cronin does too often. Brett Young was none too sure of himself as a speaker, being afraid his voice would not carry to the back of Houston Hall. He had arranged with his wife to signal to him if he should talk more loudly. She had to signal to him several times. His *Marching on Tanga* seems to me a pageant comparable to *The Flight of a Tartar Tribe.*

We have a rotating chairmanship in the Department of English and I happened to be chairman in 1926-27 when the Mask and Wig Club gave Pennsylvania $10,000 to be spent for drama. Robert Frost and Daniel E. Owen had told me about the round-table conferences at Bowdoin, and on that basis I arranged to bring five playwrights to Pennsylvania to help students of drama who wished to write plays. I wished very much to have Dunsany appear first. I regarded him as the playwright of that day who was the foremost apostle of beauty in the world. He would not come over in the fall, however, for that would miss him the hunting that he so loved. As things turned out, the course did not get under way until February 20, 1928, when Jesse Lynch Williams, a choice of Dr. Quinn, who succeeded me as chairman, began the lectures. Dunsany began his part of the work on March 19, staying in Chestnut Hill as the guest of President Gates of Pennsylvania. Dunsany did his chore well, taking more individual interest in his students than you would expect of a man with so many interests and so busy writing. He had hopes that he might make contacts here that would put his dreams of old beauty on the screen, but he could not convince the movie people of the appeal of such a project.

The winter of 1937-1938 I brought two Irish playwrights to talk at Pennsylvania, Frederick R. Higgins, author of *A Deuce o' Jacks,* and Paul Vincent Carroll, author of *Shadow and Substance.* Edwin P. Norris had got to know Higgins well on a trip to Ireland in 1935. He arranged for him to talk in class. Higgins did that well, but what I most enjoyed of his visit was his singing, to old Irish airs, many of the songs of his projected volume of verse. W. J. Phillips charioteered him out to Valley Forge with Norris and myself on the back seat. All the way out Higgins sang, in a light and high baritone. It was a drive to remember.

Paul Vincent Carroll could not believe it was all true, the success of *Shadow and Substance* as played by Sir Cecil Hardwick. The play had been a moderate success at the Abbey in the winter of 1936-1937. Eddie Dowling, looking for some play to repeat the success of Maurice Evans in the revival of *Richard II,* had the happy inspiration of taking *Shadow and Substance.* Carroll was frank to say he did not think Hardwick played the canon so well as Arthur Shields. Nevertheless, the production went over "big." I saw it in Philadelphia after a rather dubious week in Pittsburgh and liked both the play and the acting very much. After two weeks in Philadelphia the play went to New York and the whole house was soon sold out for ten weeks. The demand for tickets was so great the speculators bought up all they could for long ahead.

Carroll gave a good talk to the class in English 93, the "Irish" course. He said a great deal that I have always said, and the remarks were so close to mine some of the boys caught my eye and laughed. He told us, talking in my office afterward, that he thought England was sure to sell out Ulster for peace with De Valera. The choice of Douglas Hyde, an Episcopalian, for president of Eire, certainly looked like a gesture of conciliation to the northern Protestants.

Eddie Dowling had told us in a talk at the Franklin Inn Club that he thought he had saved drama in America from going to the dogs by his success with *Richard II* and the success that would surely come to *Shadow and Substance*. To hear "The Sunshine Boy" of musical farce, the comic genius of *The Sidewalks of New York* so talking was a wonder of wonders. To hear him tell of his rise from singing waiter in a roadhouse on the edge of Philadelphia to "dramatic impressario" with as large views for dramas as Oscar Hammerstein ever had for opera was even more amazing. There was no doubt of his sincerity in working for art, no doubt of his earnestness, no doubt of his intention to drive through to fine ends.

CHAPTER 16

HENS

NONE of my interests have been more amusing to my friends than my keeping of hens. The fact that I take them each year to New Hampshire with the family always elicits laughter. If I did not take them, there would be no cock crow in the gray of dawn on Fellows Hill. When we first summered there in 1917 there were hens on all three of the neighboring places, then in the hands of native stock. Charles Fellows had hens and Alva Batchelder and George Gray. Now there are summer people on all three places and Rolls Royces and West Highland whites, but no hens. They know our name now in the neighborhood and how to pronounce it, but for years I was "the man from Philadelphia who brings his hens along." The practice has even brought me eight lines in the title poem of Robert Frost's *New Hampshire*:

> And she has one I don't know what to call him,
> Who comes from Philadelphia every year
> With a great flock of chickens of rare breeds
> He wants to give the educational
> Advantages of growing almost wild
> Under the watchful eye of hawk and eagle—
> Dorkings because they're spoken of by Chaucer,
> Sussex because they're spoken of by Herrick.

I come honestly by my love of fowls. It descends to me, skipping my mother, from her people, her mother's people, the Reeds of Milford Mills. It descended to her brother Pliny, who delighted me in the earliest days I can recall by appearing at our house in bright March weather with a rooster under his arm. He was a firm believer in outcrossing and he thought stock was always hardier for the introduction of new blood each year. The earlier chickens I can remember at Church Lane were golden spangled Hamburgs and a blend of white Leghorns and light Brahmas that looked very like the Columbian Plymouth Rocks of later years. I can recall Uncle Pline come to us with a brown Leghorn under his arm, a golden Wyandotte, a black Spanish, a black Minorca.

I took no part in the care of the fowls on Church Lane. After we moved to Tulpehocken Street in 1878 I am afraid I bothered and hindered old Laurence by my attempted ministrations to his feathered charges. I was so interested in the fowls here I got Father to build a new chicken house for them. When we built on Upsal Street we moved our Tulpehocken Street henhouse there, but after a few years we built a long combined chicken house and tool house.

When Father and Mother died in 1907 I took over the remnants of their flock of hens, building a clapboarded house for them on Wissahickon Avenue. I had lived without hens on the place for seven years, but I was never content without them. The flock was of mixed origin but it was dominantly of golden Wyandotte stock. A single-combed hen of this variety lived to the age of thirteen years, the oldest hen I ever had. With all my experience with hens I never had had any real teaching of how to manage them. I got hold of government reports as to how to house and feed them after I acquired Father's hens and soon had the nondescripts laying better in winter than they had ever laid on Upsal Street.

My quest of the red Dorking, seemingly the fowl the Romans brought to England, I have written of at length in *The Wissahickon Hills,* in an article called "The Famous

Dorking Fowl." I still have a little flock of these spangled beauties. We still ship three crates of fowls to Mt. Whittier each June and three crates of them back again to Germantown in September. Most of our young birds are raised in midsummer in New Hampshire. The large grass yards in Sandwich and the plenty of insect food in them set the hens laying wildly soon after we arrive there. The youngsters, too, thrive there, though we lose some of them nearly every year through the depredations of the marsh hawks. Once I have seen a goshawk after the old fowls and once a young eagle in the brown plumage.

My first reason for keeping fowls is my pleasure in caring for them. They have been about the place on which I lived, or on my father's place, where I could visit them, all my life. I like their busyness and brightness, their eyes so full of quick concern with food and freedom, the way they crowd past you when you let them out for an hour before nightfall to pasture on the lawn, their matronly self-sufficiency and pride in increase, their glad gratulations on having laid an egg, their content in mothering their chicks. I like the cock's gallantries, his alarums over passing crow or hawk, his squiring of his dames over the green lawn. I like the confidential chatter with which they greet you as you shut them up for the night, hens and cocks alike. I like cock crow in the middle of the night as a meteor flares across the sky and wakes the watchful fellow, or as full moonlight persuades him it is day and he should be leading his little troop out to breakfast and the duties of the nests. I like best of all his subdued and muffled crowing in the gray of dawn, a sound as intimately connected with my childhood as robin song or the cooing of doves, as the far cawing of crows or the lowing of cows.

The gathering of eggs has always brought me a quiet happiness. Eggs have always seemed treasure-trove to me, whether it was when I gathered them as a great privilege granted me in childhood, or as a duty when I took over full charge of the chickens at Father's, or whether it was as a relaxation after the long day's work in town, after dinner and to the accompaniment of lantern light in the black night. I remember a winter's morning when I took Mrs. Frost and Robert out to see my Dominiques. It was in those years I had more time to spend on the fowls than I have today. The clapboard house was snug with the snow piled up about it. Its floor was deep with litter of straw and leaves. The half of the Dominiques were crowded in under the laying bench and roosts above it. Every one of the seven nests had a hen upon it and into one a second hen was trying to crowd. These were all but all pullets, hatched from eggs set on New Year's Day, and now in their prime of thirteen months. I think they, both the Frosts, wondered could a college professor take proper care of hens. I remember Mrs. Frost saying, in a sort of an aside to Robert but with a half-amused glance at me: "It is evident he knows how to do for them. There will be plenty of eggs here today."

I am well aware that the care of hens seems a very plebeian calling to some people. They just cannot understand why Uncle Pline stayed on at Milford Mills in Chester County with his grandmother because he could not tear himself away from his Dominiques. I met a former student of mine one Friday noon as I was coming from a poultry show in Philadelphia. He said: "Ought you not be going to the orchestra?"

As I was on my way thither, I said: "Yes, I ought to be on my way there, and I am on my way."

He looked at me a little quizzically and said: "I see." What that "see" meant was: "Isn't a visit to a poultry show a strange prelude to listening to symphony music?"

Years afterward when we were more of an age he recalled the incident I have related and said: "Will you think me rude if I ask you if there is another man interested in both hens and music?"

I said yes and fairly inundated him with names, beginning with John Cope and ending with Tito Schipa. I followed that up by hurling at him *The Golden Cockerel* of Rimski-Korsakoff and that movement of Moussorgsky's *Pictures at an Exhibition* that gives the dance of chicks breaking from their shells.

As to writers so interested, their name is legion. Thoreau is very laureate of cock crow and hens' cackling. Before him there are Herrick and Walton and Chaucer. Since Thoreau's day we have the henhouse episode of Stevenson's *St. Ives,* and Masefield's many references. Masefield has given us the passage about buff Orpingtons I have referred to, "poultry stricken grass" in *The Daffodil Fields,* and that reference in "Autobiography" in which he had good talk in "Bloomsbury nights" with Synge until so late an hour "the barber's cockerel crew." Frost was a successful breeder of white Wyandottes, but it is Langshans he celebrates in *North of Boston,* in the eclogue called "The Housekeeper."

My interest in hens has led me into correspondence that has revealed to me much of country life both in England and America. Mr. Fitch-Hogg, of Essex, has returned to finish a letter to me, after throwing a bootjack out of the window to quiet the nightingales so he could think to compose his periods. This he gravely explains in a footnote, to account for a swerve in his penmanship. One year, on our way from Sandwich, we made a detour to Coleraine in northwestern Massachusetts to visit a breeder of Dominiques. Had it not been for Dominiques I had **never** known this country of apple orchards and covered wooden bridges.

Without my own breeding of Lester Tompkins' Rhode Island Reds I had not understood the development from them of New Hampshire Reds, a breed whose winter laying has pretty nearly revolutionized the hen business in northern New England. I had known less of Philadelphia Quakerdom without good talks re Dorkings with John Cope of Awbury. Without my many visits to Simeon Yerkes on Limekiln Pike I had known less of the Pennsylvania artisan-farmer. Without my interest in Jersey Black Giants I had known less of Burlington County over in Jersey than I now know. My interest in hens has been the "open sesame" to me of half a dozen countrysides I had else not known.

CHAPTER 17

WRITING

WHAT power over words I have I owe initially to three sources, the talk of Laurence Kelly, the prose of the Old Testament, and the prose of Thoreau. It was my reading of the poets, from the day in youth I wakened to the lyric world of Wordsworth on through those years of young manhood in which I discovered Yeats, that enriched my vocabulary and taught me that writing must be lyrical if it is to be able to cope with the expression of those intimate moods that are the heart and soul of literature.

It was the talk of Laurence, a talk obviously handed down the generations, that taught me that writing should be simple and direct and sinewy, that it is the better for being objective, concerned with matters that have come home closely to the business and bosoms of men. Laurence was without any of the self-consciousness that underlay what we were afterward to call self-expression, and yet so effective in his straightforward speech and so picturesque of phrase many resayings had stripped bare that I was early persuaded that the traditional ways of expression were the best ways. There was rhythm, too, to his speech, a rhythm very different from, yet just as marked, as the rhythm of the King James Bible.

We did not have Bible reading at home, and I did not go to church very much, only when I had to. Yet there was much reading of the Bible in school and in Sunday school, if not always of those parts of scripture best as literature, and what times I did go to church I was driven to reading the Bible and the hymnbook through the dullness of the sermons. Only the talks of returned missionaries held my attention. I was interested in the wonders of the world's ends they incidentally revealed. It was the Psalms first delighted me. Having to learn this or that one by heart, I discovered a rhythm in their prose that was pleasant to the ears as the rhythm of the hexameters of Vergil and Homer I had to scan in school were pleasant.

After the Psalms I found my way to Proverbs and The Song of Solomon and Ecclesiastes. Childhood has its troubles, and youth, and I found a tonic philosophy in such declarations as "to the hungry soul every bitter thing is sweet." "Remove not the ancient landmark which thy fathers have set" delighted my backward-gazing disposition. The rhythm of "in the twilight, in the evening, in the black and dark night," and of "the words of the wise and their dark sayings" fell on my ears like a benediction. I was then in the state of mind that held with Yeats that "only words are sooth."

There was revelation for me in a passage in one of Thoreau's journals, perhaps *Early Spring in Massachusetts,* in which he records how he sat on a stump in a rainstorm and felt as if he were a pen held in the hand of nature. "I am the rain and the grass and the atmosphere writing." That has echoed and re-echoed in my ears ever since. No words about writing have meant more to me and have been taken closer to heart. I conned over and over *A Week* and *Walden* and fairly devoured his journals. I did not play "the sedulous ape" by keeping a journal of my own but I did take to heart his admonitions that there is everything to be interested in wherever you live, provided, of course, that it is a country place.

Another book that was of great interest to me for its material, but that had not much to teach a tyro in style, was *A Naturalist's Rambles about Home* given to me by my father at Christmas of 1884. That deepened in me the conviction that one's proper concern was in one's own back yard.

I had not formulated as yet the theory of writing I was to preach from the beginning of my teaching at Pennsylvania in 1897 on to today, "The Higher Provincialism." I was beginning, though, to write in earnest and to practice what I preached. Both the poet and the novelist I most revered in those days had written of their own folks and their own countrysides with an art of the center, an art followed long in English poetry and in the English novel from its beginnings in Fielding. Wordsworth was a "higher provincialist" and so was Hardy, whom we did not know as a poet until 1898.

I dimly sensed by the mid-nineties that what one should do was to find a little world of his own undiscovered before he came upon it, and write about that. I cannot now recall when I began to call my theory "The Higher Provincialism," but, perhaps, by 1902, when my study of "The Higher Provincialism" of the Irish writers led me to Ireland. The Gilbert White whose Selborne I visited was another higher provincialist. I had written out-of-door essays in accordance with that principle. "The Glittering Hills" (1902) to be found in *The Wissahickon Hills* (1930) had to wait twenty-eight years to see the light but others were in print from 1904 on.

I had not realized I had been born with ink in my blood when I began to try to write. I knew Grandfather Thomas had a knack of turning graceful album verse, that he Scotched it after the manner of Burns, and that he wrote an admirable letter. I did not know that my father's grandfather, Cornelius N. Weygandt, and his great-grandfather, Jacob Weygandt, had run German newspapers in Easton. I knew that Father had kept a diary from 1848 and that he was still keeping it. Not until his death in 1907 did I know, though, how full it was. He had never shown me any passages in it or read from it to any of us. It was all a great secret, and the writing of it a labor of love. I know now he felt its contents too frank and explicit to be revealed.

It was the urge to write sent me into newspaper work. I was lucky to get out of it before it had so tired me I was fit for nothing else. It taught me to drive through to a finish, and at one sitting, even considerable hundreds of words. It taught me a great deal of life. It taught me much about the theater and about book reviewing. It taught me directness and concreteness and not to drool things out. It taught me to come quickly to the point.

It did not teach me what I had begun to guess from listening to Laurence, that a great deal of the best writing is what is overheard. My walking about the country and going to country auctions had brought me into contact with all sorts and conditions of men from crowders and charcoal burners to drovers and ministers, from pineys in New Jersey to "potentates goodly of girth" in San Diego, from Portuguese on Cape Cod to Pennsylvania Dutchmen on Plum Creek, from New Hampshire farmers to Philadelphia lawyers. From all I have heard picturesque phrases and stories well worth repeating but more stuff I could use in my writing from the humbler sort than from the sophisticated. It was in Clementon in New Jersey the proprietor of charcoal pits said to me of one of his workmen: "He wouldn't farm for a farm." It was a Pennsylvania Dutch woman returned from Philadelphia for a week end on the farm of her birth who said: "The boys can go barefoot now the bumblebees are out." It was my neighbor in New Hampshire said to me: "The pine ain't like the oak or the ash. The pine won't bear any grief." It was a college professor reverting to the folk speech of the countryside where he was born who said of pastures growing up to brush: "The poor man's birch and then the pine."

My first book, *Irish Plays and Playwrights* (1913), was all but all of it written when I was thoroughly tired out with teaching. Its one chapter I can have some pride in is that on Synge. That chapter took me the whole ten days of an Easter vacation. The other parts of the book were written, most of them, late at night after I had studied my lessons for the next day. I am so constituted I have to read over all my notes for a lecture before I give it. I have to read, too, something of the man I am to talk of over again before I can talk convincingly of him. I have everything written out to the last detail, but I cannot read a lecture. I have to know it well enough to talk it. I have to have my quotations by heart. If I read them the lecture drags. As it is my teaching I am paid to do, I have to do that first. In forty-eight years' teaching I have had six half-years off, or a total of three years instead of the seven the sabbatical year every seventh year should have entitled me to.

There was no other book until there came *A Century of the English Novel* in 1925. That came out of more than a quarter-century's lecturing on the novel. It is a better book than *Irish Plays and Playwrights,* but not on so fresh a subject. The claims I made for Yeats in my first book were held too large by some reviewers, but time justified them. Yeats was given the Nobel Prize, and there was no quarrel with the title of my book on contemporary British poetry, *The Time of Yeats.* The death of Kipling left him unquestionably the first British poet of the day.

Tuesdays at Ten (1928), so far as I know, was the first book written by an American college teacher for his old students. Another teacher must have had a like intention in mind for shortly after my book another of like purpose appeared. There are whole lectures in this book, set down almost exactly as I talked them, articles rewritten in less compass than a lecture, for magazine publication, illustrations from life of points made in the lectures, asides and runnings off at tangents. There were but 1,250 copies printed, 250 signed, and it is now out of print. It brings in bits of all the sorts of writing I have done, out-of-door stuff from Pennsylvania and New Hampshire, memories of my trip to California in the summer of 1923, criticism, incident, familiar essay, a formal address trying to explain the precise qualities that make our University of Pennsylvania what it is.

I had been planning *The Red Hills* (1929) for nearly forty years before I wrote it. While I was a boy in college the hope came to me that someday I might write a book about the Pennsylvania Dutch as I knew them. I was about three-eighths Pennsylvania Dutch by blood. I had heard stories all my life about my father's people, of Easton and its Delaware and his old aunties who lived in the Forks City. I had gone to Lebanon as a boy in days when you heard no English spoken on the streets. I had made many expeditions to various parts of Dutchland, both before and during and after my newspaper years. I had written an editorial on things Pennsylvania Dutch while I was on the *Evening Telegraph* that brought the paper letters of protest and of approval. I read Elsie Singmaster's stories from the date of their first publication. I had read Ulysses Koons about Ephrata. I had read Governor Pennypacker's articles. I knew Martin Grove Brumbaugh well. I had sat at college under Oswald Seidensticker. It was he who began the serious research into our origins.

All our characteristic buildings appealed to me strongly, covered wooden bridges harking back to Switzerland, and those bank barns that were known commonly as Swiss barns; ground cellars and springhouses; the layout of the villages on hilltops with the long and narrow strips of land reaching back a mile or more; the quaint attire of our Plain Clothes people, Dunkards and River Brethren, Mennonites and Amish; the Easter services of the Moravians; roofs of red tile and decorated platters of redware pottery; the Indian bridges made of a great tree felled across a stream and adzed flat on the top; the illuminated writing to be found in birth and baptismal certificates and house blessings—the hundreds of items that so sharply distinguished the "Dutch" culture of Pennsylvania.

I would reiterate that I insisted in all my writing and speaking on "Pennsylvania Dutch" rather than Pennsylvania German. I was delighted to find out when the Pennsylvania German Society was founded that "Pennsylvania German" prevailed over "Pennsylvania Dutch" by a majority of but two in a vote of more than fifty. I believed in calling ourselves Pennsylvania Dutch because that was what the world called us. I was pleased to find that three out of four of the old travelers who wrote of us in English called us Pennsylvania Dutch. It was my friend, M. G. Brumbaugh, who, as I have said, tried to fasten Pennsylvania German upon us and who succeeded insofar as the bulk of scholarly writing about us is concerned. He believed it would remove an inferiority complex from a people whose English was often laughed at. "Insist on being called Pennsylvania German," he said. That insistence on Pennsylvania German had only the effect of further increasing the inferiority complex of the "Hillmen," the poorly educated folk of the remote places in the mountains. It made many of the educated Pennsylvania Dutch ashamed of their own people. Pennsylvania German is as I have said, a phrase got by pedantry out of an inferiority complex. I am proud I have given that phrase a setback. Most of the writing about us that has any tang and savor about it calls us "Pennsylvania Dutch." It is "Dutch" food the cookbooks celebrate; it is "Dutch" tables and kitchen cabinets the auction lists advertise; it is "Dutch" pretzels you buy in Lititz or Ephrata.

The Red Hills gave Dutchland heart. After the barn symbols were written of approvingly in *The Red Hills* they began to come back on the barns. Many more folk were interested in spatterware and redware and painted chests and illuminated writing after they read of them in *The Red Hills*. "The first book about us that does not laugh at us at all," said a Reformed clergyman to me. But the highest praise of all came from that scholar who said: "Weygandt, damn him, has put back for ten years the general acceptance of 'Pennsylvania German.'" Weygandt is proud to believe he has put that obnoxious term back for twenty years. Pennsylvania German reeks of the lamp— I would emphasize that again and again. There is no hominess about it, or picturesqueness, or romance, or earthy savor. If I say it who ought not, in *The Red Hills* we who are Pennsylvania Dutch put our best foot forward.

The Wissahickon Hills (1930) is a bird book. I was born just over the divide between the Wissahickon Valley and the Wingohocking Valley, on the Wingohocking side. In 1878 we moved to Tulpehocken Street. The little creek in the meadow behind us ran into Papermill Run and Papermill Run ran through Rittenhousetown to the Wissahickon. I tramped the Wissahickon Hills day in and day out at all seasons of the year from 1878 until 1900, when I came to live where I live now right on the hills above the Walnut Lane Bridge. I learned of their trees, their flowers, their birds, their beasts, and the record of that learning is the book *The Wissahickon Hills*. Every morning from late September until late June I look out upon those hills. My concern for them, that they should escape the hands of those who have constantly despoiled them, one let us say by uprooting their moccasin flowers and fringed gentian, and another by tearing down their old mill buildings of stone, and a third by neglecting and then removing the Livezey's Lane Bridge, led me to make a plea for the last covered wooden bridge remaining in all our Philadelphia countryside. "The Friends of the Wissahickon" saved the Thomas Mill Road Bridge.

A Passing America (1932) has to do with covered wooden bridges and red cedars; with Venetian blinds (which have come back); with katydids and tree toads; with quill pens and Dominique hens; with Catherine pears and supper; with coach dogs and Germantown wagons; with daphne odora and Quaker bonnets; with chestnut trees and purple martins; with log cabins and Greek; and with oxen and feather beds.

The White Hills (1934) is a book of out-of-door and familiar essays, and people and picturesqueness in the New Hampshire that has taken nearly all our summers since 1912, when Clarence Child steered us to Birch Interval above Wonalancet. We bought a farm on Fellows Hill in Sandwich in 1916 and we have had at least ten weeks there every summer save in 1923, when I taught summer school at the University of California at Berkeley. This book brought us a good many visitors in the summer following the spring of its publication. It awakened as much interest in New England as *The Red Hills* did in Pennsylvania. I found myself being accepted as an interpreter of New Hampshire despite my name so distinctively Pennsylvania Dutch. Its successor in 1937, *New Hampshire Neighbors,* so far confirmed my true-blue Yankeeism that I was invited to write the introduction to the W.P.A. guidebook *New Hampshire: A Guide to the Granite State* (1938).

I had been taken in by the neighbors in Sandwich after

about three years of summer residence there, 1917-1919, but it was not until 1924 that I was entrusted with the Old Home Week sermon in the Baptist Church in the Centre. I have New England blood in my veins, of Athertons and Swifts, and that may account for my fitting into so different an environment than that I was born to in Pennsylvania. New Hampshire has never seemed a strange land to me. I have motored to all parts of the state, so that I know as much of it as I know of my native state. There are, of course, but two cultures of the old stocks in New Hampshire, English Puritan and the nearly allied Scotch-Irish. There is altogether less to be learned of its dwindling people than of populous Pennsylvania. The good speech of the countryside, however, helped me greatly in my writing, and I have come to love the northernness of the landscape and to make many friendships with the people, friendships that have endured. All New Englanders are more of a reading people than we of Pennsylvania and the appeal of my books about New Hampshire is relatively wider, considering the number of people in the state, than the appeal of my books about Pennsylvania in Pennsylvania.

In my third New Hampshire book, *November Rowen* (1941), my title is taken from a Sandwich neighbor now dead, Loveland Hines, who was always saying: "There be no hay so sweet as November rowen." Rowen is aftermath, second crop, and Loveland's creatures seemed to bear out the truth of his saying. The rowen spent well and his cows gave milk all winter. It is really my third crop from New Hampshire, a book of my old age, and its title is so lovely of sound I could not forego it even if it would not be understood widely outside of New England.

The Blue Hills (1936) is a better book about Pennsylvania than *The Red Hills*, though it has not the latter's specialized appeal. It is a book about all the stocks of Penn-

sylvania, not about the Dutch alone. The last item in it,
"From the Forest of the Night," is as good as anything I
ever wrote, as good as "Rain on the Roof" in *The White
Hills*. My book considers British Quakers and Scotch-Irish
as well as the Pennsylvania Dutch considered in *The Red
Hills*.

We are great borrowers of books in Pennsylvania, especially those of us who are Scotch-Irish or Pennsylvania
Dutch. An old couple in Hilltown in Bucks County read
The Red Hills, the copy being lent them by their city son.
A picture of a symboled barn in it, the very spit of their
barn, added to their desire to have the book. They got so
far as taking the money necessary out of their secreted
horde and putting it in a jar on the end of the mantelpiece.
They were Mennonite farmers who did not often get to
town. They were apt to go to Wanamaker's when they did
get to the city. They were told the book could be bought
there. I doubt if they have bought it. Two years after the
four dollars was set aside for the purchase of the book it
was still in the jar on the end of the mantelpiece.

I had been eight years working on *A Century of British
Poetry*, a companion volume to *A Century of the English
Novel*. It turned out too long for one volume, and, despite
valiant efforts at rewriting, it could not be brought into
the compass of one volume without all the life squeezed
out of it. So *The Time of Tennyson*, Volume I virtually of
A Century of British Poetry, came out in the fall of 1936,
and *The Time of Yeats*, Volume II, in the spring of 1937.
They were little advertised and reviewed at much less
length than my earlier critical books, *Irish Plays and Playwrights* and *A Century of the English Novel*. They were
better books, both of them, than their predecessors of like
kind, for I had read more poetry than plays or novels. I

had read, in fact, nearly all of the poetry that mattered written in Great Britain and Ireland.

My purpose in the two volumes was to write of British poetry from Tennyson to Ruth Pitter as it appealed to America. The American background is always insisted upon. In my library I had the eighteenth-century poets that my mother's father read, Pope and Young, Collins and Gray, Bishop Percy's *Reliques* and Burns. I had my father's Shakespeare and Milton, Coleridge and Shelley, Motherwell and Browning. I had bought the late Victorians and Neo-Georgians as they appeared, Henley and Hardy, Kipling and Watson, Phillips and Yeats, Housman and Hodgson.

The fact that I am a Philadelphian of Philadelphians informs all of *Philadelphia Folks*. I laugh at myself and the people of our city and suburbs as I laugh at most things in life, in good humor and without malice. I pay the city and its people the compliment of believing it and they can stand being laughed at. Only the other night I heard Professor John Milton Fogg, Jr., humorously explain our Philadelphia conservatism by the fact that we live in that part of the States oldest geologically and botanically, in Alleghanian America. Though our rows of houses are shot full of holes by buildings torn down to avoid taxes, though we are overrun by hordes of Negroes from the South for whom there is no proper housing, though scores of our industries have been taxed out of the state, though we were hard hit by the depression, Philadelphia is still essentially the Old Philadelphia, the city of homes, the city in which every man long resident either owns his own house or is looking forward to owning it. The old stocks are sound to the core here, folks of Hollandish descent and Swedish, British Quaker and Pennsylvania Dutch, Scotch-Irish and New Englanders and Virginians.

My writing has been in intention of two sorts, critical writing that has come out of my teaching of the English literature of Victorian and Georgian and Neo-Georgian Britain, and essays familiar and out-of-door, that have come of my concern with the American countryside as I have known it in Pennsylvania and New Hampshire. I have, too, found a new way of writing of antiques, of which my Rose Day address at Manheim is an example. Instead of talking only about Baron Stiegel and his glass, I followed the use of the rose as a decorative motive and as a symbol through all Pennsylvania Dutch interior decoration and artisanry. This trail leads beyond glass to fractur and painted tin and punched tin, to inlay on clocks and other furniture, to decorated Easter eggs and butter molds and so on through the whole gamut of home art.

My writing has in it the accent of the spoken word. It has almost all of it been said before it has been written. A large part of it is based on speech overheard. Much of it, too, is in a sense a collaboration. A waiter in the Reading Terminal restaurant in Philadelphia gives me the phrase "latticed tarts" for pies of open top with strips of pastry overlaying the top. Jesse Ambrose, of Whiteface Interval, brings me the story of "The Maine Man and the Minister." Levi E. Yoder, of Silverdale, gives me the story of "Enos Keyl's Cow." The bootblack at Thirtieth Street Station tells me of the wild rabbits close by on bare ground in the heart of town.

Many of the phrases in my New Hampshire books are from the lips of my neighbors Charles Fellows, Alva Batchelder, Frank Bryer. So it is only natural that my writing has in places something of the aphoristic quality of folk speech as, for instance, in the phrase: "Hay is not all that withers into sweetness." Again it reveals some sweep of imagination such as comes to lonely watchers of the skies, as in "All you are aware of is the world of glittering stars, and their radiance, soft and cold, falling through unrealizable space, on you, an atom, watching them." There are many people in all my writing, some of them limned at full length, some of them only sketches. There is catching of the genius of place, the tang of the soil, atmosphere, an intense awareness of the skies overhead, at broad noon, at day's end, at midnight full of stars.

18

HUNT

HE WAS such a gentleman, for one thing. He was so friendly and demonstrative for another. He was so big and bounding and full of life. He was so much more happy in my company than was anybody else. He was, of course, a dog, "damned by a dog's brute nature to be true." He came to us as a puppy in 1925, when he was six weeks old. He slept under my bed each night until that evening when we took him off, faint with pain, to be freed from that pain by the veterinarian's needle. I thought that the automobile had brought more joy into my life than any new thing could bring after one is forty, but Hunt, only the last of our dogs, no new thing at all, brought me more fresh joy when I was past fifty than I thought so late years could bring.

He was with me in those years in which I began to grow old. I felt no aging at all until I was fifty-five. I was as quick on my feet until then, despite visitations of this or that form of rheumatism, and as sound of wind and limb, as I had ever been. But age will not be denied. I felt myself slowing up physically, and, in some slight degree, mentally as well. Lines of verse I had once had in memory were less ready to my tongue, names of characters from books and incidents in their stories were not always present in memory when I wanted them. More and more teeth were going, the avoirdupois was steadily increasing despite the good deal of exercise I still got in.

I daresay my temper was getting shorter. I am not the best judge as to that. I could still hold the attention of audiences in talk, and of that larger audience one meets through books. I was, in fact, still growing in power over words. As to personality—I do not know. Perhaps the appeal of that was lessening. Certainly I was less and less disposed to commerce with my kind, I who never was given to social functioning. I was clearheaded and realistic enough to recognize that I was going downhill. Hunt stood by me. He was just as glad to be with me, even if in the summer at Sandwich I could not take him any more on the long walks that so delighted him. Every morning he went with me for the milk to Mr. Fellows and every morning he made the fuss over Charles that delighted the old man.

He would rush out and bark at strangers, but save in the rarest instances that barking ended in gracious greetings, tail waggings and jumpings up on the visitor. As he grew older he did not like other dogs on his preserves, but he never, after he was five years old, got into any serious fights. He was never a gadder. He had his rounds in the immediate neighborhood, visits to this dog and that, grave meetings with slow tail wavings in most places, play with one spayed bitch, a diminutive wire-haired fox terrier. Twice a day, perhaps, he visited round, but most of the time he stayed at home.

While he was still a young dog he generally spent the evening with the family in the living room, but as he grew older he often went upstairs by eight o'clock and crawled under my bed. When he would hear me turn over above him, he would thump on the floor with his tail, to let me know he was standing by in the darkness of the night. There was a sense of protection in his presence that I never had with any other dog, terrier or spaniel. He was a Labrador retriever, the son of a mother who came from England, the child of her old age, but sturdy and little visited

HUNT, LABRADOR RETRIEVER

THE WEYGANDT SUMMER HOME IN SANDWICH, N. H.

with ills until the trouble with the prostate gland that made his end inevitable.

In Germantown he had only squirrels and rabbits to chase and an occasional bobwhite or ringneck. At Sandwich there were all sorts of fascinating savors, of bear and deer, fox and raccoon, weasel and mink. Best of all there were woodchucks. He was a proud dog when he came in with one he had caught unaided. The most he got he chased into stone walls. In such instances, he summoned the family by his barking, and we dug the most of them out for him to kill. It was only when he had a freshly killed woodchuck he was cross. Once or twice in such circumstances he snapped at some member of the family. Sometimes, too after he had crawled under my bed for the night he resented being hauled out. He seemed to regard that retreat as his den and growled if you stuck your hand in to pull him out by the collar. He would always come out cheerfully enough, though, when you called him.

As he grew easily carsick we never took him to Sandwich with us in Ford or Chevrolet, but shipped him in a great crate lined with two thicknesses of cellar window wire. In one shipment, when he had been got by mistake on board boat at Boston for Philadelphia and was shut up without food for four days, he had all but gnawed his way out when he arrived home late one Saturday afternoon. In the last few years he was seldom more than twenty-eight hours in his box, arriving home about four in the afternoon after leaving Mt. Whittier the noon before. Leaving Germantown about five one afternoon he would be out of his crate at our house in Sandwich by four the next afternoon. If we did not arrive until the next day he would stay happily in the dooryard and go up to Charles Fellows's for his meals and stay there the night.

I used to worry a good deal about the shipping of him,

but that worry was as nothing to the pleasure I had from having him about. It is impossible for any human being to be so long devoted to another human being as a dog is to his master. Hunt's devotion never slackened all the eleven years he was with me. After one such devoted beast has died one is slow to give one's heart to another. One fears "The Power of the Dog." One remembers "Dinah in Heaven" and wishes it were as true as it is beautiful. One must in the end leave all he loves with no "four feet trotting behind."

I feel so strongly about the power of the dog, of the place he should hold in the affections of men, the sincerity and whole-souledness of his devotion, that I just cannot understand the right kind of people not liking dogs. I have to admit I have known two good men who did not like dogs. I have known only those two. When I hear a man say that he does not like dogs I write him down at once as a poor sort. He may not, of course, so be. But further knowledge of such a man generally reveals yellow streaks in him. Someone will be remembering W. H. Hudson's attack on the dog, but that is partly but a desire to differ from the crowd, not a real revelation of the writer's lack of ability to appreciate fineness. Loyalty is one of the first qualities in life to me. It is not cynicism that leads me to say that such loyalty as a dog has for his master is not possible for human to have for human. In this attribute the beast has the better of the man.

CHAPTER 19

BIRDS AND BIRD SONG

THERE are those who will say: "He cannot have had many sorrows, if the death of a dog is among the first of them." It is true that the death of Hunt took more happiness out of my life than has any other incident in that life. The loss of happiness is not exactly sorrow, but it is close to sorrow. I have, of course, had the usual disappointments, failures to accomplish what I would, slippings away of what I had set my heart upon. All my years since boyhood I have had but the one ambition, the ambition to write, to reveal my own state of Pennsylvania as the richest, culturally, of all the United States. I have, in a measure, fulfilled that ambition, and that has brought me some satisfaction. Always, though, I look to what I have left undone. That and not what I have done concerns me first. I have taught for my living because I could not make a living by my kind of writing, and no kind of writing of what people would pay for has ever meant anything to me.

I have been successful in teaching. I have drawn large classes because I can talk, because I correlate all literature to life, because I can make my points in a way that burns in and is remembered. I have done this teaching with all of me and it pleases me to know that it has counted in the lives of many who have sat under me. Fan letters and visits from people who have liked my books have been pleasant, too, but I have had no joy in such matters comparable to that I have had in fellowship with Hunt and in listening to bird song.

In early May of 1938 the wood robins returned. For five

years and more we had not had them daily on the lawn and singing from the sassafrases and oaks about the house. They were a vigorous and bouncing pair, quick in their motions for wood robins, with only occasional lapses into the quiet dignity of most of their kind. I had never known a pair of wood robins so alive, I had never heard a wood robin sing so well as the cock of this pair. It was a full-voiced song, clear, resonant, oboe-toned. It spoke to me of valleyed peace, it was a benediction sweet of the honeyed half-light of many-columned woods.

I saw the birds on the lawn on Sunday, May 29, in superb beauty and vitality. The cock sang all day long from dawn through the twilight. That was the last I heard of him or saw of either of them. Although I had heard another wood robin answering him in the neighborhood I heard no wood-robin song on Monday or Tuesday or Wednesday. Our place, that had been ennobled by that song, was just the acre of pleasant countriness it had been these five years it had failed to re-echo with wood-robin song. Light, wind, boscage, blue sky and clouds, plastered house of warm sand from the Wissahickon, items that made the appeal of our place, were lacking that final touch that transfigured it, that "outlet" song of life, as Walt Whitman called it.

What had happened to the pair of wood robins I have but a poor guess. They must have been nesting, they were about so long, three weeks and more. Did a crow find the nest and filch its eggs? Did a cat or hawk catch one or the other of the birds? Not to have them about with the cock singing was a blow. A something had gone out of life, a something less than the death of Hunt, but a something that was a large loss.

I relate the incident to prove how much bird song, and,

above all bird songs, this particular song of the wood thrush we call locally wood robin, has been to me.

It is because of their songs, of course, that birds have from early childhood appealed to me more than any other part of the out-of-doors that has been more than half of life to me. As a child I made collections of their eggs, though never taking a full set. The years subsequent to childhood have brought few moments of joy to me comparable to those I had when as a small boy of seven I climbed the ladder-like limbs of the Norway spruces in front of our house in Tulpehocken Street and looked down on the green eggs, brown splashed and black splashed, deep in the nests of the blackbirds. The books call them purple grackles but they were blackbirds then to all who knew them through birdlore handed down the generations rather than through identifications of them made possible by the bird books.

Aunt Rachel and Uncle Pline were full of talk of the country home at Milford Mills they remembered so clearly from childhood. There were there killdeers and whippoorwills and purple martins and many other birds we did not have about Germantown. Older boys, some of them rather disreputable, hunters with the killers' instinct, extended my knowledge of birds considerably. Dad Darrach helped me, too, climbing great oaks in the Wissahickon woods for crows' eggs and hawks' eggs. I read Wilson and Audubon and Nuttall, being particularly interested in them because all three wrote of birds observed in or about Philadelphia. As I have said already, Witmer Stone was a big boy at the Germantown Academy when I went there in 1882 as a boy of ten. He got me to join the Delaware Valley Ornithological Club when I was a boy in College. From 1890 to his death in 1938 I knew him well. He was available for explanations and help of all sorts when I ap-

pealed to him. Appreciated as he was for his long service
to the Academy of Natural Sciences, and honored as he was
by his fellow ornithologists, he was never appreciated as
he should have been. When I spoke at the banquet of
Pennsylvania alumni on March 8, 1935, on the occasion of
my name being written on the silver cup of the University
of Pennsylvania Club of New York City, I mentioned
Witmer Stone. A guest, a Cornell man who had been
brought to the dinner by a Pennsylvania man, a friend of
his, came up to me at the speaking's close, and said to me:
"I am so glad you paid tribute to Witmer Stone. I do not
understand why everything is not made of him everywhere.
He is the first ornithologist of America and one of the few
wholly just and true men humanity has produced."

That has always been my feeling about him. To me he
was as surely the foremost Pennsylvanian of our time as
Stephen Foster was of day before yesterday. It was not, of
course, until his *Bird Studies at Old Cape May* came out
in 1937 that he achieved a book worthy of him. There is
no book about birds in America to put alongside of it. It
reveals as kindly a heart as that of Gilbert White, a power
over prose akin to that of W. H. Hudson, a knowledge
that is greater than that of any of our great ornithologists.
The book has not been accorded the praise it should have.
The museum ornithologists who have reviewed it did not
recognize it as an achievement in writing, they did not
know his presentations of herring gulls and white-bellied
swallows were poems in prose. Always heard in this writing is the voice of the sea, always haunting it is the mystery
of the sea, always there is breaking out in it some bright
beauty of light on white egret or glittering stretch of thor-
oughfare. Wafts of salt air and of air sweet of the pines
wander through its pages. Kindly faces of old seamen ap-
pear and disappear. The inexplicable in bird ways is can-

didly admitted. Scientific fact lies down with romantic wonder as quietly as lion and lamb on the old plates of "The Peaceable Kingdom."

I make special expeditions to visit swales where the wild crab apples break into pink beauty and scent all their neighborhood with utter sweetness. The fringed gentian pulls me to meadows along the upper reaches of French Creek. Tulip poplar and locust delight me on my own acre. Shad bushes are a lure to the hills along the Susquehanna and dogwood bloom calls me to a hundred woodsides. Birds, however, come one after another into one's dooryard. One can hardly dress of May mornings for the warblers in the trees about the house. The scarlet tanager nasally announces his arrival from the high tops of the black oaks, where he is joined now by golden oriole and now by rose-breasted grosbeak. The ringneck brays from the moundtop next door, the crows are always noisy in the offing.

The catbird is always about the rhododendron hedge. Three pairs of robins are on the lawn almost any time you look out on it. There are chimney swifts circling high over the place off and on all day, and wildly tossing and wildly crying nighthawks in the evening. We have, too, the city birds about us, starling youngsters larger than their parents following them about over the shorn grass, and English sparrows and pigeons. The field sparrow's voice comes to us from the hayfield back of our house and the wren's chatter. Life would be much less worth living to me without these birds about.

In the summer I am lucky enough to be able to hear wood robin and hermit thrush and veery from our own acres. There are herons in the sky over Sandwich, and black duck, and once in a while a goshawk or an eagle. There are ruffed grouse in our woods and pileated woodpeckers and a vociferous tanager, the solitary vireo, the rose-breasted grosbeak and wandering flickers. There are many sparrows in the open fields, white-throats always calling, pewees, bluebirds, barn swallows, chimney swifts, and white-bellies. We are never out of hearing of Maryland yellow-throats, chestnut-sided warblers, and ovenbirds. It is perhaps the bluebird's warbling means the most to me of all these bird songs for the bluebird is all but gone from the Wissahickon Hills where I spend three-quarters of the year. Sometimes I think I have more joy from the barn swallows, which talk to me so confidingly when I open the barn door of mornings.

The birds come to you, you do not have to search them out to see and to hear them. That is to say, very many of them do. The woodcock in Sandwich probe nightly about the water barrels and pitch themselves up in marvelous evolutions down by the water hole in the north woods. The shore larks settle down on the burned-over berrying ground. The hummingbirds work off their surplus energy describing great U's above the foxgloves. The chipping sparrows creep like mice through the low grass on the lawn. The yellow-bellied sapsucker beats his tattoo where you can watch him on the porch peak. The vesper sparrow makes the great roof of the barn a sounding board for his faint far-carrying song.

Of course if you would see the snow geese at Fortescue you have to make pilgrimage to southermost Jersey. Or if you would see the swans on Chester River you must spend the night in Chestertown to catch them before they are off for the Chesapeake by dawn. It is all the snow geese that are, some ornithologists think, that pass a fortnight on Delaware Bay on their way north, fourteen or fifteen thousand of them. There may be miles of swans, thousands of them, talking all night off Chestertown, making such a din you can hardly sleep.

Great flights of hawks all day passing, two thousand white swans in the air against blue hills across Chesapeake Bay, a flock of blackbirds that obscures the sun for ten minutes and more, ducks that all day long fly up from your train eastering from Victoria—these are great wonders, but the little sights you come on day by day are more productive of joy. They lead you to expect another little wonder on the morrow. Driving to town one day you see two wood duck fly almost straight up from Wissahickon's bank to a tulip poplar limb thirty feet above them. You see a red-winged blackbird settle down on a crow's back just outside of Chestertown and the crow light on the ground to rid itself of its tormentor. You see seven black-headed gulls skimming like great swallows up Susquehanna above Harrisburg. You watch California quail marching in line like geese across the campus at Berkeley. You watch a robin, just once out of a hundred instances, drive away a starling nagging it on the lawn before College Hall of the University of Pennsylvania. You remember that undervoice and eerie song of the gray-cheeks among the gray rocks and the dark green spruces on the summit of Whiteface. You remember the crested tits' loud monotony from the budding pear tree by your house. You recall the stunned indifference of the vireo you picked up from the porch floor after he had flown into the glass of the porch end. You remember the orange warbler the cat brought into the summerhouse at Schannos on the Raymondskill.

It is their songs, though, that count for most, their songs and their cries. The whippoorwill that by chance calls in our lane on his way to places in which he nests, that call brings back all the far places in which you have heard it.

That cooing of doves that comes to you through the gray of dawn as you lie abed—there is peace in it and sleepiness and heartsease. You would give a good deal could you hear again the rollicking song of the Carolina wren, gone now these five years from the Wissahickon Hills. The catbird sings and sings and sings, dreamily, ecstatically, matter-of-factly, running through a wide range of emotion. The robin chorus is everywhere in the background and one bird in full song from the ground under your window. A song sparrow is uttering his simple notes from somewhere way off. Beyond all and over all, though, rises the chant of the wood robin, impassioned, cool, full-voiced, with pleading in its oboe notes, the song that, for all the long years you can remember it, has been to you the first of bird songs.

CHAPTER 20

THE MEANING OF ANTIQUES

ONE could not spend five years in the German-town Academy without coming to care for the beauty of its old building of 1760. It is built of our "Germantown stone," the "stone with a glimmer," as the Swedish naturalist Peter Kalm called it, a gray mica schist with green tones running through it. The lines of its exterior are good and its trim and moldings inside as they should be. It is a "colonial" building, as were the many similar old houses that made Germantown Road a place of distinction in the days of my youth. That we have allowed those old houses, so many of them, to be torn down, is but another proof of the decay of American taste in these last hundred years.

Certain heirlooms, come down in Father's family, the Augustine Neisser tall case clock, a Windsor chair my grandfather made, the portrait in oil of Great-Great-Uncle Jacob Weygandt, the straight flutes made by Grandfather Weygandt, appealed to me because my people had made or owned them. So did the ball-and-claw-foot mahogany table that had come down on my mother's side, a woolen comfortable in brown and blue, the Thomas family Bible. The Empire bookcase containing my grandfather Thomas' books was another link with the past. I found it listed in the inventory of Great-Grandfather Isaac Thomas' estate, made in 1815. The extravagant prices paid at the disposal of my great-aunt Ann Buchanan's parlor set and other items at the auction held after her home was broken up were a revelation to me of the value of old furniture.

As the years wore on and I grew familiar with Uncle

Seal's collection of chests and bureaus and porcelain pipes kept in a back-yard shop in Lebanon, I came to realize the attractiveness of old things both as objects of art and as museum pieces. I have never lost my sense of the difference of the two categories. Spatterware in soft paste and in stone china, made with peacocks and tulips on it in central England for the Pennsylvania market, red and yellow redware pottery, the illuminated writing known as fractur, these items of interior decorative objects held dear in Dutchland are some of them beautiful. I like many such items that I should never call beautiful. I can like them for quaintness or primitiveness even if they are not beautiful.

The furnishing of our little house in the Wissahickon Hills in 1900 from the antique shops in Philadelphia's Pine Street added to my knowledge of the interior decoration of yesterday. The house itself was homemade in 1844, peasant made, by Germans from south Germany, but a good deal of the furniture we bought to put in it was of an artisanry that reached almost to art. I began to go frequently to auctions a decade later, and today I am the survivor of literally hundreds of them. I have, too, made the rounds of antique shops over all southeastern Pennsylvania, and of a good few in New Hampshire and Maine.

I have a large collection of redware pottery today. I have, too, much china, many baskets, a share of ironwork, a good deal of brass, wood carvings, painted and punched tin, glass from Pennsylvania and South Jersey and from Keene and Stoddard in New Hampshire, objects in bone and horn and tortoise shell, slat-back chairs, zitters and dulcimers, old manuscript music books and all sorts of pictures, in oil and needlepoint and tinsel. It is my familiarity with all these forms of interior decoration that is the basis of my knowledge of the superiority of the taste of four generations ago to our taste today.

The account books of country stores, the sales books of potteries and glass houses, the lists of books taken out of libraries all confirm this judgment. We have not gained taste through education to take the place of that we lost through the decay of tradition. I cannot declare too often that it is only in conveniences such as plumbing and heating and lighting, in medicine and sanitation, and in transportation, that we have advanced.

I have a good deal of the old woodenware, much of it stained red with madder. I have chopping bowls and churns, noggins and drinking mugs, candle holders and salt boxes, knife cases and spoon racks, candlesticks and cats' troughs, sugar buckets and butter kegs, saffron boxes and egg cups, sanders and calipers, T squares and foot rules. With old planes picked up at country auctions Son got out moldings for our old house in New Hampshire, which is the best antique we own.

Through talks with fellow collectors, with antique dealers and with auctioneers, I have added to my knowledge of yesterday. These men have conjured up for me the apparel of old times, its boots and embroidered waistcoats, its high hats and hair dressing, its kerchiefs and gowns, its cloaks and mantles, its silks and fine array, its vanity boxes and fans, its greatcoats and smockfrocks.

I have visited all the shops that I have learned of where old trades are practiced: the pottery of Jacob Medinger in "The Stone Hills" of Pennsylvania; the basket weaving of Jonathan Moses in the Connecticut Valley in New Hampshire; the fork and rake shop of M. B. Young in Lancaster County, Pennsylvania. I treasure ox goads and turkey bells; straw beehives and mats of cornhusk; brick molds and sieves of horsehair; girting chains to measure cattle and crude mole traps; copper cocks for weather vanes and brass apothecary's scales; cider kegs and great pestles and mortars; wooden shovels for handling grain and apple parers; hearthstones of marble, and pothooks and trammels.

It is the diaries that I have picked up at country auctions, and the church record books, that tell me most of yesterday, though old folks have handed on to me much information by word of mouth that might be gone on the wind did I not write it up. There are those, of course, who believe that yesterday is negligible, that all our concern should be with tomorrow. I have found in every art of which I know anything, in every science, in every political, social, and economic condition, there can be no progress save on the foundation of the past. My chief interest in all antiques is in their beauty or picturesqueness or in the sense of comfort and well-being they bring about the heart. I cannot forget, though, how important a knowledge of antiques of all sorts is for the general culture of the future. They are a large element in making our world worth saving.

CHAPTER 21

FOLKLORE AND THE FOLK ARTS

ALL my life folklore and the folk arts have been close at hand. It was, I suppose, from his father, born under "The Blue Mountain," that my father heard the phrase for snow falling: "The Bluebergers are plucking their geese." It was from Aunt Rachel I heard rhymes about the signs of weather, of the meaning of "mare's tails," or "mackerel sky," or "rain before seven." She repeated again and again: "A red sky at night is the sailor's delight; a red sky at morning is the sailor's warning." From her I had it that spider webs on the lawn meant a clear day, that wind kept off frost, that mud was good for bees' stings.

As I have said, Laurence Kelly brought me up on rhymes of Brian O'Lynn and on tales of Dean Swift and his man Jack. Irish maids and Irish-American maids from the coal regions of Pennsylvania added various bits of Gaelic folklore. It was *Uncle Remus*, perhaps, that made me listen attentively to Frank Ellis, who had been so trusted as a slave in Virginia he was the custodian of the keys of the smokehouse on his master's plantation. It was he who told me dreams would come true if you told them to your wife before you rose up of mornings and that roast possums should be stuffed with chestnuts and sweet potatoes. Moreton Cummins had many Br'er Rabbit stories, but it was Mr. Rabbit in his versions. He had dreams of being an angel and flying down for dips in the sea of warm milk there was in heaven.

As early as 1888 I heard ballads sung at East Waterford

in Juniata County, but I was more interested then in town ball and birds and tales of bounty jumping in the Civil War, and I neglected to learn all I might have had I been aware of their significance. As a child I had not realized that the ribald rhymes cast at us as we walked east to school on Church Lane in Germantown would one day be of first interest to me as folk song. They were sung at us, because Quaker children were of our group, and Quakers were considered proper game by the juvenile humorists.

In the 1920's trips upstate in Dutchland brought me many tales of untoward signs, such as the visit of a snowy owl to a window sill portending death to one in the house, and of fabulous creatures, phantom dogs, hoop snakes, and dragons. The dragon of Hiester Hollow in Berks lived on hogs and flew always west to east. The dragon of Crystal Cave was killed by a soldier returned from the Spanish-American War. It was now I learned at firsthand of hexes and powwow men and how firm a grip their practices had on the hillmen in back-country places in Dutchland. It was a real surprise when I began summering in New Hampshire to find that witches had just as firm a grip until yesterday on the life of middle New Hampshire. A spotted fawn running breathless into a graveyard was supposed to have taken over the soul of one for whom a grave was being dug. An eagle soaring above an old man being committed to the grave had a whole community in awe of they knew not what. "There is more belief in witchcraft up Russell Street," said one of the best men I know, "than there ever was in Salem of Massachusetts." I have heard of country schoolteachers, taking courses in state teachers' colleges, believing in "absent treatment" of hated persons by melting wax images of them. A hundred years ago pigs on a neighboring farm to ours in Sandwich danced on their

hind feet in a ring about a man who had refused to marry
a witch's daughter down in Weare.

I have written in detail in *Down Jersey* (1940) of fiddlers and ballad singers in and out of "The Pines." Elven
Sweet lived at Magnolia, out from Pemberton, when we
visited him five years and more ago. He lived in a typically
Jersey house of clapboards. Playing at parties brought in
some of his income, but he was a cranberry picker and
master of half a dozen kinds of odd jobs. He had once, he
told us, over two hundred tunes in his memory. "I've
played right through the night on dark winter evenings
and midnights and small hours, from dark of one day to
dawn of another, without repeating a tune." He judged
we would like best the old tunes and gave us "The
Chicken Reel," "Miss Macleod's Reel," "The Devil's
Dream," "Up the Road to Lancaster," and Foster's "Oh,
Susannah."

Elven Sweet's home was by the side of the road in open
country. The home of Harvey De Camp was back from the
road in the heart of "The Pines." He played, on a fiddle
of tiger-stripe red maple his father had made, "The Devil's
Dream" that Elven had played, "Trotting Horse" and
"Pop Goes the Weasel." I have never met a higher cour-
tesy than his. After his playing, I said to him: "How can
we ever repay you in any way for the pleasure you have
given us by your playing?" His reply was: "You have paid
me for it by enjoying it. Come again and I'll be glad to
play for you again." And this was after he was sorely dis-
appointed by the purpose of our visit. He had thought I
was a dance-hall impresario from some coast resort come
to hire him to play in his place. That was a new identification of me.

Stacy Bozarth, the ballad singer, lives right in the village
of Budtown. Elven Sweet took us there one Sabbath morn-

ing, but too close to the dinner hour for us to hear many of his repertoire. He began with "The Cuckoo," who "sings as she flies." "The Jolly Sailor," that goes to a rousing air, followed, and the ribald "Bachelor's Hall," and "The Banks of Roses." Stacy sang by ear, and by ear Elven and Harvey played.

The New Hampshire ballad singers that I know are Amos Linn Chase, "the bard of Atwell Hill"; Jonathan Moses, of Orford Street; and George Royal Brown, in Tamworth, on the road from Fowler's Mills to Chocorua Pond. Amos writes vigorous satiric verse, of which "The Back-Farmer's Harness" is an example, and narrative verses like "The Flintlock," which recites an early settler's troubles with bears. He is a picturesque man with a full beard, whose rheumatism has driven him to crutches, but who still has the strength and determination to cultivate a large and productive garden. He plays the bones with vigor, using them to emphasize his songs of Negro minstrel sort. He acts out such verses as "The Sugar Place" in pantomime. These verses put poignantly the feelings of the old man in seeing cut down the sapwoods where he had sugared as a boy.

Amos sang us the widely distributed American ballad of "Jim Fiske," and an old English ballad, "The London Girl." He was, though, naturally more interested in what he called his histories, such verses as "The Flintlock," "The Sugar Place," "Jim, the Farmer Lad," and "The Skillet." These were most dramatically sung, with elaborate gestures and coloring of voice to bring out the emotions underlying the incidents they record.

Jonathan Moses confines himself to old ballads and to the popular songs of fifty years ago. The ballads from over the Atlantic are his long suit. To hear him sing "Squarrie Lampman," which is "Lambkin," or "Brandon-on-the-

IN THE HEART OF DUTCHLAND, OLEY VALLEY

STIEGEL GLASS

FRACTUR AND PAINTED WOOD FROM
PENNSYLVANIA DUTCHLAND

Moor," is to have memories that last down the years. He is a big man of seventy with a merry twinkle in his eye. He has at least fifty ballads by heart, words and music both, besides the songs he knows. I had known him as the maker of the best splint baskets I had ever seen before I discovered by accident that he was a ballad singer. His repertoire was learned from his father and mother, Vermonters both. It was a big family, eleven of them, father and mother, three boys, and six girls, and the ballads helped to pass the time as they all were in the shed, setting up baskets. They lived in one place, Weybridge, say, until they had it "basketed," and then moved on to Castleton, working there until all the neighborhood was fully supplied with baskets of brown ash, and then moving on again.

Like Amos Linn Chase, Jonathan Moses puts on a good show. He had great success in the summer of 1942 singing some of his favorites over at Bread Loaf in Vermont. Among the ballads he sings are "Johnnie Scot," "The Dark Orchard," "Sweet Sixteen," "The Butcher Boy," "The House Carpenter," and "Lord Bateman." He has a queer power of taking you in imagination away from the Connecticut Valley of today to some lonely place oversea in the Scotland of long ago.

George Royal Brown has the best tenor voice I have heard off the operatic stage. Well toward eighty, he is still possessed of a voice full and strong, subject to every modulation he would give it. He has sung for Clifton Lunt and me a song in praise of the hills of old New Hampshire, a song in the tradition of the Hutchinson family; what called itself a "chanty" on the death of a "dark-haired lad" in breaking a log jam in a Maine river; "The Robber's Song," an old ballad; and "Long-Waisted Peggy," which he calls a "rattler."

He told us that he had his "living from the woods," that

he and his dogs did well on hedgehog meat, that he had killed over fourteen hundred hedgehogs and nineteen bears. He was born in Portland, Maine, the son of a sea captain, and raised among his mother's people on a farm on Stacy Mountain in Madison. He is proud of his ability to "dovetail" logs in building a log cabin. By "dovetailing" he means so notching the logs at the corners that the adzed surfaces will fit snug one to another without being chinked with stones and mud and moss. According to local belief there has never been a better woodsman. He is a commanding figure now in his old age, with grizzled beard and long mustachios. There is an independence and dignity about him that compel respect. Time was he was an accordion player of parts. With his voice and powers of talk he brings many callers to his shack almost in the shadow of Chocorua. He can conjure up for you all sorts of scenes, the bringing in of a bear, its skinning and butchering; the shooting of a deer at an incredible distance; Jim Liberty building a log barn; the singing of a chanty to a hushed audience in a Maine lumber camp of fifty years ago.

It has been one of the most treasured privileges of my life to have known as a living thing this heritage of old verse and song handed down the generations, to have heard talk that proved its talkers "rude poets of the tavern hearth," to have met literature in the memories of men as well as in the written word embalmed in books.

CHAPTER 22

THE DECLINE OF OUR MORALE
AND CULTURE

THE PHRASE "a reading of life" is George Meredith's. I have made use of it for years in teaching analysis of literature. Has the writer considered the gift of telling a story? Has he the art of characterization? Has he the gift of putting truths about life in so brief and telling guise that, once heard, his dicta can never be forgotten? Robert Frost is full of such observations: "a decent product of life's ironing out"; "the best way out is always through." Many such readings of life are desolating enough, such as George Moore's about life being a poor thing, "an old hat to kick down the road." We have all been brought up on such declarations. This one is from the Bible: "Sorrow is better than laughter." That one about man's ingratitude, from Shakespeare. Another from Sir John Davies, of Hereford, declares man is a "proud but yet a wretched thing." With the parrot's memory I had in youth I had stored up so many of such declarations that I could justify a rather pessimistic philosophy of life by quoting them one after the other.

I was for all that, though, an optimist, my definition of whom is one who believes seven out of every twelve issues in life come to right conclusions. I have always told the boys in class that you must not lose your faith in human nature when your best friend stabs you in the back. I have always told them, too, to beware of anyone to whom you do a favor. The reason a man will not forgive a favor is obvious. His pride is mortally wounded because he cannot win his battle with the world without assistance.

I have known favor, of course. I was put on the local staff of the *Philadelphia Record* because my father had been a fellow student with the proprietor of the *Record* at the Philadelphia Central High School. I was given a place in the English Department of the University of Pennsylvania because I had been a boy with a responsive face in the classes of Professor Schelling and because I had done fairly well in courses in English. At the *Evening Telegraph* Watson Ambruster had supported me loyally when I had made "breaks" not to the newspaper's interest in this matter and that.

My independence of attitude, and my want of pliability in the hands of managing men, and my disinclination to take executive office have been resented in various organizations of which I have been a part. I have had my differences with my colleagues in college but few serious ones. I have never had any axes to grind. I have never wanted anything from Pennsylvania but more money and leisure.

I have not found it wholly true that one is without honor in his own country, but I have had more recognition for my writing in New England than in Pennsylvania. Teaching and writing are held in higher regard north of Boston than round about Philadelphia. I have been told when asked to speak in Philadelphia "free, gratis, for nothing" that they were paying two hundred dollars to a New Englander because Philadephians liked to listen to outlanders rather than to inlanders. And that happened just after I had crowded the Lincoln Room at the Union League, which holds pretty nearly, I am told, a thousand people.

Things in most respects have grown worse in my lifetime. The men of my generation, men of three score and ten, have more loyalty, more independence, more kindliness in them than the men of fifty, many of whom were broken by the First World War, and much more than the men of thirty, broken by the depression of 1930-1940, and by being forced into relief by the government. There is infinitely more pettiness in life than there was, almost nothing of tolerance and largess of spirit left, an envy of one's neighbor the greater opportunities of yesterday prevented.

For thirty years I have felt and said that most of American life, save in comforts and healthfulness, save in the gains made by preventive medicine and surgery, has steadily deteriorated for more than a hundred years, that we have less taste than our forbears of 1830-40, that despite two generations of trained architects, American cities have grown uglier year by year. There were signs for a change for the better in this respect, a return to the Grecian temple style of public buildings and to Georgian houses, but the bungalow and the Tower of Babel modernistic styles have set back the better day that promised.

It has been my large concern with antiques, antiques in the largest sense, that has taught me of our deterioration. I know Monticello and the quadrangle of the University of Virginia, Chestertown and Newcastle and Williamsburg, Hope Lodge and the Chew House in Germantown, and scores and scores of old houses by Connecticut and Merrimack, in Portsmouth and in Wiscasset, San Juan Capistrano and Carmel and San Diego, Carpenter's Hall and the Statehouse in Philadelphia, and manorial homes and beautiful cottages in inland places all over our eastern countryside. I know interior decoration of all sorts, old glass, old silver, old portraiture, old furniture. It is because I know of all these things and have collected as many of them as is possible for a poor man to collect that I can justify my statement of our deterioration. Our taste began to lapse when we broke with tradition. The family gives its children much less today than the family gave its children in the 1830's and the 1860's and the 1890's, to consider but three generations. The sons I now teach of parents I taught a generation ago come to college with less cultivation than their parents had. I must say again that no college teaching can compensate for what family tradition once gave and now fails to give.

It is too soon to tell what will be the nature of the recovery of civilization, if recovery there be, from the Second World War and its revelation of the atomic bomb. One seeks refuge in the old adage: "Hope for the best; be ready for the worst; take with calmness what God sends."

CHAPTER **23**

WISSAHICKON AND WHITE HILLS

I HAVE been fortunate in the homes I have had. I can remember, of course, nothing of my birthplace on Walnut Lane, a neighborhood still suburbia after more than seventy years of the town growing up about it. We moved to Church Lane when I was one as I have said, and during the next six years there I grew into an awareness of those things that are still of first interest to me. When we lived there this neighborhood was almost as open as farmland. There I learned to know wood-robin song, and the pale orange and green flowers of the tulip poplar tree, and that hens were not just hens but golden Hamburgs and light Brahmas.

There I first began to tag at the heels of an old Irish gardener, Daniel McCarthy, and to hear Irish rhymes and picturesquenesses of speech. There Aunt Rachel began to tell me tales of the hill farm in Chester County where she and my mother were born, and to instill into me that love of country things that is so close to my business and bosom. Farm wagons passed on their way to market, one so full of country produce its driver was forced to drive seated on its front step with his feet down on the singletrees. I remember well his shaven upper lip and stubbly beard, his trousers forced down into knee boots, the sleeves of his red flannel undershirt protruding beyond his coat sleeves as if they were wrist warmers.

Thirty years afterward that man's grandson boasted to me he was as near an aristocrat as America had produced. He said this to me just as I was leaving him at Wayne

Junction. I had only time to get off the train, so I could not recall for him that picture of old time. Curiously the "aristocrat" has just such attitudes and motions and gestures as has many a rheumatic old farmer.

It is curious to me, to whom a farm life is that which is preferable to all others, to find so many people believing it is necessarily a dull and uncultivated existence. It has been resented when I have said in public addresses that few Americans of my generation are more than a generation from the farm. One woman said that her people had always been professional men, ministers and lawyers and physicians, and did not thank me when I said I had seen her ministerial grandfather plowing his glebe land in Connecticut.

We moved to West Tulpehocken Street in 1878 and we lived there ten years, the last years of which saw me a freshman and sophomore at the University of Pennsylvania. We moved to Upsal Street late in 1888. That place of five acres was virtually farmland, with an old cedar-bordered lane running through it that was one of the dividing lines between the long strips of land in which Germantown was laid out. The original settlers built their houses on Germantown Pike, the houses perhaps a quarter of a mile apart. From this pike their land ran back in narrow strips two miles and more to the Wissahickon Creek. Father's place was no more than a half mile from the Chew House, where "The Battle of Germantown" was fought and lost by us in "The War of the Revolution."

It was here I began to try to write about birds, birds of the neighborhood, birds made familiar to me on trips to the Berkshire Hills, to the Jersey coast, to the White Mountains. It was here I lived through my last years at college, my newspaper years, and the first years of my college teaching of English, which began in 1897.

When I married Sara Matlack Roberts, of Germantown, in 1900, we went to housekeeping at 6635 Wissahickon Avenue. We are there still. The little old house, built by Pfeils from the Rhine Valley, in 1844, we enlarged by a wing, but it is still but a little nine-roomed affair. They built the house out of stone quarried close by, and out of black oak timber cut on the place. The walls were plastered with sand dug from the Wissahickon Creek a half mile away. The house was but a six-roomed one, with solid stone walls, with no air space in them. We rented the house first, and bought it eight years later, with almost an acre of land.

To the southeast of us was Hong's Woods, a woods a quarter of a mile broad and more than a half mile long. About us were open fields. Great black oaks by the lane overshadowed the house. There were many trees on the place, mazzard cherries and sassafrases chiefly, lilac bushes and box bushes close by the house. It was so open country when we came here in 1900 we could see but four houses from our dooryard, an old house built by the Rittenhouses, and long lived in by John Welsh, minister to England under Grant, across the way, and three houses built by his married daughters to north and northeast of us.

Our hilltop acre looks westward to the Wissahickon. Though we are less than seven miles from the center of Philadelphia, there are rabbits and gray squirrels about in numbers, deer mice and ground hackies. There are opossums in the woodpile, and a friend has seen as late as 1944 a raccoon crossing the road as the headlights of his car picked up the creature making his way home to the Wissahickon woods. One morning recently the lady of the house saw a red fox in the heath bed.

There is wood-robin song here at the right time of the year, from late April to early August, and the faint ven-

turing of the wood pewee in early evening, catbird song
and thrasher song, song of song sparrow and robin. Hawks,
great Cooper's hawks, sharpshins of moderate size and thinly
crying sparrow hawks are about. Screech owls hunt for
snowbirds at winter nightfalls in the English ivy on the
house. Ten times in forty-five years I have seen eagles
passing. Herring gulls come up Wissahickon from the
Schuylkill and cross our place on their way to the Delaware.

Our house harbors old furniture, much of it come down
in my family or milady's, a chest of drawers of crotch walnut, a Chippendale chair in mahogany, a high chest of
drawers inlaid with tulips, slat-back chairs, a Sheraton sofa,
old china made in England for the Pennsylvania market
that we have gathered in a hundred trips upstate, Pennsylvania Dutch pottery and fractur, books galore. Little house
and little place tell of the taste and interests of their oc-
cupants and make a safe retreat from the ugliness fast
pressing in on all sides from a deteriorating world.

Our summer home in middle New Hampshire is another quiet harbor. On a hilltop encircled by mountains it
looks out on Ossipees and Sandwiches, with their many
memories of Whittier and Thoreau and Frank Bolles. Here
survives a rhythmic speech on the lips of the oldsters. The
low house of white painted clapboards is staunch enough
to float away should the waters rise in flood out of the
near-by valleys. It was so typical of the farmhouses of the
state a picture of it was chosen for the front cover of a circular gotten out by the state planning commission to at-
tract people to New Hampshire.

In Sandwich we have become a part of the life of the
community, but my native Pennsylvania has given me
much more than New Hampshire could. It has, with its
seven old cultures, so much more to give than New Hamp-

shire, which has but two old cultures, English Puritan and
Scotch-Irish, to give. I know New Hampshire well only
from June to October, so three seasons and its people's
rounds of work in late fall and winter and early spring
have escaped me.

In New Hampshire, though, I have had more leisure
than in Pennsylvania, and it is hours of leisure that bring
us the fulfillment of life. I can say this, who hold that work
is the greatest thing in the world. I have had time in our
summers on Fellows Hill for many kinds of requiting
work. I have piled rods of wall here. I have, with my son,
built a piazza ell to the house so like the old part visitors
think it is a converted woodshed. I have hoed here, and
dug potatoes and brushed and burned brush. I have written much here, and rewritten it, with the echo of the fine
speech of the countryside in my ears. I have listened to
more good talk here from backwoods folks than I have
heard in any city. I have had time to get to know people,
in their homes and in our home, at auctions and before
and after church, in roadside colloquies, and at nooning
when we all were resting from labor.

Three of my four books about Sandwich I have mentioned. The other is *The Heart of New Hampshire* (1944).
This book is full of people, neighbors near and far. Here
survives the America of yesterday, men and women not all
ironed out by the steam roller of industrialism into flat
uniformity one with another.

What a pageant they would make could I conjure them
up before you, men living and men from the shades. Save
for Isaac Graves and John B. Hoag, I am almost the oldest
inhabitant now. Oldster after oldster has passed on to me
the traditions and stories, the avocations and pastimes of
a world gone from us, a better world than that in which
we exist today.

It was Charles R. Fellows, my next-door neighbor, wrote me the best letter I ever received, beginning, "The plums are just blown and the apples in red bud." A little man and a merry, with chin shaven clean and flowing side whiskers, and inimitable as a storyteller, his high heart never lowered when adversity threatened in old age. "We shall have to take it as it comes" was his philosophy of life.

Frank A. Bryer, the best cryer of an auction I ever listened to, was another master of our mountain speech. His talk of November landscape and Morgan horses was poetry talk. He was so fellowly a human being that he, a Democrat, was sent to the state legislature in a town two-to-one Republican. Alva W. Batchelder talked me a lyric of the cow, which made her a "rural divinity" as surely as the essay of John Burroughs. George Gray you would never want to stop as he talked of the cuckoo, "a little brown bird cries the whole of July," or of lining bees, as he let the flowering stem of goldenrod slip through his fingers.

Uriah McDaniel the bear hunter; Wes Tewkesbury, who could do anything with oxen; Larkin Weed, master builder; Hiram Corliss, basket maker and hater of "bannocks"; White Penniman, whom the beavers plagued; Ed Currier, with his record of racing horses on the ice of Ossipee Lake; Loveland Hines, he who said "There be no hay so sweet as November rowen": their like we shall never see again. I could go on in such fashion about another score of my neighbors. I have, however, written of them one and all elsewhere, and I must now have done. They have helped me to put on record the closing days of as fine a civilization as our country has known, a civilization of which they were survivors from our heyday a hundred years ago.

THE RECORD TO DATE

WELL, that's the record to date. I have had a busy life, the common experiences and a few that are less common. I have been able to do what I set out to do years ago. I have so written of our state of Pennsylvania that it is recognized as it was not before *The Red Hills, A Passing America,* and *The Blue Hills.* I have widened the horizons of thousands of students and I have given them charts to steer by.

There is still work ahead. There is writing I want to do will occupy me until I come to the end of my tether. There will be, I suppose, that physical shrinking from death all flesh is heir to, but I do not care to live longer than I can be of use to my family or to my little world. I have had enough of many things in life, of the city, of the theater, of lecturing. I have not had enough of writing, of listening to music, of country contentments. I hope I am privileged to live on the Wissahickon Hills to the end. I could not be happy where there are houses just across the street and lack of elbow room about the house. The little things, as all my life long, are still the most of life to me.

My solid satisfactions are now in the visits of birds to our place, a pair of red-breasted nuthatches, a pair of crested tits with the male singing; and in my knowledge there are rabbits in the heath bed, and possums in the woodpile; in cock crow in the night and in crows calling in the dawn, in the rush of wind through the leaves and in moonlight silvering hoar frost on the lawn.

INDEX